The Dancing Fox

ARCTIC FOLKTALES

"The other girl pointed to a whale skull and said, 'This one will be my husband'"

The *D*ancing Fox

ARCTIC FOLKTALES

EDITED BY
John Bierhorst

ILLUSTRATED BY
Mary K. Okheena

William Morrow and Company, Inc. • New York

Text copyright © 1997 by John Bierhorst
Illustrations copyright © 1997 by Mary K. Okheena
All rights reserved. No part of this book may be
reproduced or utilized in any form or by any means,
electronic or mechanical, including photocopying,
recording, or by any information storage and retrieval system,
without permission in writing from the Publisher.
Inquiries should be addressed to
William Morrow and Company, Inc.,
1350 Avenue of the Americas, New York, NY 10019.
Printed in the United States of America.
Design and typography by Jane Byers Bierhorst.
1 2 3 4 5 6 7 8 9 10

Library of Congress Cataloging-in-Publication Data
The dancing fox: Arctic folktales / edited by John Bierhorst.
p. cm.
Includes bibliographical references.
Summary: A description of Inuit culture accompanies a collection
of eighteen Inuit folktales from an ancient oral tradition in which
animals could take human form and in which magic usually had a part.
ISBN 0-688-14406-3
1. Inuit–Folklore. 2. Tales–Arctic regions. [1. Inuit–Folklore.
2. Eskimos–Folklore. 3. Folklore–Arctic regions.] I. Bierhorst, John.
E99.E7D33 1997 398.2'089971–dc20 96-17146 CIP AC

Contents

Introduction

A vast treeless region stretching across Alaska and Canada and including all of Greenland, the American Arctic is the homeland of a people who share one heritage and who increasingly have come to be viewed as one nation. Often spoken of as the "Eskimo," the people are called *Inuit* (IN-oo-it) in their own language, in their own publications, in their dealings with other nations, and in world councils.

As the twenty-first century begins, the Inuit leave behind the traditional skills and methods that have enabled them to survive for thousands of years in the Arctic environment. Today the igloo and the dogsled have been replaced by the carpenter-built "matchbox" house and the snowmobile. Electricity has made the oil lamp a relic of the past; and settlements once isolated at the extreme limits of human habitation are now connected by air travel, fax machines, and satellite TV to other parts of Inuit territory and to the world of the "Southerners" far below.

Nevertheless, traditional values remain essential to the modern Inuit community. These values are expressed in the continued use of the Inuit language and in the still-widespread harvesting of Arctic foods. The old values also find expression in Inuit music, Inuit graphic art, and, not least, in the recollection of Inuit folktales. Language, food customs, music, and art are important ways of keeping in touch with the world of classic Inuit culture. But it is the retelling, or rereading, of the old tales that brings this world to life.

The storyteller

Since the middle of the twentieth century, remembered folktales, especially in Canada, have been written down and published in Inuit newspapers and magazines, often side by side with news stories. Many of the publications are bilingual, either Inuit-English or Inuit-French.

In Alaska, folktales appear in books prepared by Inuit tellers and, in some cases, Inuit editors. These are published by the Alaska Native Language Center in Fairbanks. Unlike the Canadian publications, which remain in local communities, books brought out by the Native Language Center are distributed worldwide.

In recent years, as occasions for live storytelling have become rarer, the tape recorder has been used by older people to preserve tellings of folktales for children and grandchildren. Sometimes it is possible to bring together a few listeners, whose expressions of amusement or surprise help to re-create the atmosphere in which the tales were originally told.

In the old days, however, a gifted storyteller could entertain an audience of twenty or more persons with dramatic tellings that lasted hours into the night, often to be continued night after night. Vivid descriptions of these sessions have been preserved by two prominent collectors of nineteenth- and early-twentieth-century Greenlandic tales, William Thalbitzer and Gustav Holm.

In the words of Thalbitzer, "Each hamlet had its great narrator, or perhaps several masters in the art—old men or women—who, in the long winter evenings, if nothing more festive offered, would begin to relate, and from his or her place between the skin hangings of the platform, and while silence fell over the listening group, hold them spellbound with one tale after another."

According to Holm, the storytellers' performances were marked by "gesticulation, shouting, and modulation of the voice," and "their dramatic skill is often so great that a spectator can follow the story even if he understands only a few words of the language."

With this kind of performance in mind, an Alaskan storyteller once admonished the great explorer and recorder of Inuit folklore Knud Rasmussen: "You ruin our stories entirely if you are determined to stiffen them out on paper. Learn them yourself and let them spring from your mouth as living words."

The power of the word did not depend, however, upon gestures or facial expressions. In western Canada the lamp would be snuffed out at the beginning of the session, and as people settled into their beds they listened in total darkness.

An unusual method of delivering stories has been reported from eastern Canada, where it is said that the teller used to sit down in the rear of the house and tell the story slowly and solemnly with his face turned toward the wall. Deliberateness also marked an old Alaskan method, which called for a storyteller's helper. During the performance the helper laid out sticks as chapter markers and interrupted to correct errors.

According to old-time Inuit narrators from Alaska to Greenland, there were two kinds of stories: ancient and recent. Those regarded as ancient were the folktales in which animals could take human form and, in general, magic played a role. Tales of this sort tended to be widespread, with variants from communities hundreds or even thousands of miles apart. Stories spoken of as recent were those that recounted the experiences of relatives and acquaintances within living memory. Such tales were usually local.

The eighteen stories selected for this book may be placed in the "ancient" category, even though a modern detail (such as an iron pot) occasionally crops up, and even though one of the tales, "Two Dried Fish," is actually borrowed from European folklore. Of the eighteen, three are known from Alaska only;

four from Greenland only; six from both Greenland and Canada; and five from all three regions (Alaska, Canada, and Greenland), spanning a distance of five thousand miles.

The natural world

Winter in the Arctic is a time when there is no daylight whatsoever. Above the Arctic Circle, along the 70th parallel, the sun disappears below the horizon on November 24 and does not reappear until January 18. Not surprisingly, then, stories were told mainly during the winter season, for the purpose of making the long darkness pass more quickly.

In Greenland storytellers often ended a tale by saying, "Now the story is finished, and the winter has gotten shorter." Or, more modestly and with a note of resignation, "There, that's the end of the story, and the winter is none the shorter."

The Arctic darkness is not entirely unrelieved, however, since the spectacular northern lights may be seen practically every clear night, especially in early spring and autumn. The quickness with which the displays appear and disappear was proverbial with storytellers, who could say, "Then the entire village set to work so busily that one might have thought it the flickering of the northern lights" ("Cannibal Village"). Or, "They all ran out of their houses with the speed of a shadow cast by the northern lights" ("The Dancing Fox").

After the sun reappears in late winter, the turnabout from total night to total day proceeds rapidly. By May 18, along the 70th parallel, the sun is in the sky continuously, and night does not come again until July 28.

Thus the significance can be appreciated when the Inuit narrator says, "At last the days lengthened" ("The Blind Boy and the Loon"), or, "Before the days began lengthening again" ("The Woman Under the Sea").

When the days have once again become short, the sea freezes from shore to shore, often for six months or longer. During this part of the year the smooth sea ice facilitates long-distance travel either on foot ("Two Sisters and Their Caribou Husbands") or by dogsled ("Cannibal Village"). Only in summer and early autumn, when the sea has thawed, is it possible to travel by boat ("The Lost Boys," "The Adventures of Kivio").

In summer the sun shines twenty-four hours a day, but it stays low in the sky. As a result the frozen ground, or permafrost, thaws to a depth of no more than a few inches. Therefore the great Arctic plains, or tundra, can support only a low covering of small plants. Grass, moss, and such shrubs as heather, crowberry, and Arctic willow are among the most common plants, and all these are mentioned in the folktales.

Yet the Arctic environment supports some of the world's largest mammals. Baleen whale, white whale (or beluga), narwhale, walrus, seals, polar bear, and caribou (also called rein-deer) are among the important species. Some, like the caribou, can be hunted only at certain seasons; by contrast, the seal can be hunted in open water during the summer or, during the winter, at breathing holes, or blowholes, in the ice. All the larger mammals play roles in folktales, along with such smaller species as wolf, wolverine, and two kinds of fox, the red fox and the white-furred Arctic fox.

Birds also make appearances in stories. Among the most typical of the Arctic are the snow partridge, also called ptarmigan, and a kind of auk called dovekie, or ice bird. Both species are valued for food. Most frequently mentioned, however, is the raven, a common scavenger around settlements and hunting camps, usually treated in folklore as sinister or ridiculous.

The art of living

Although it was possible to gather berries for food, small shrubs for fuel, or moss for a lamp wick, the old-style Inuit way of life–carefully depicted in the folktales–did not depend upon plant materials. The absence of wood in particular prompted elegant solutions to everyday needs.

Whale ribs were used to frame a house. In winter an entire house could be built of snow. The intestine, or gut, of a seal made the windowpane. Cooking fires were fueled with blubber.

And slabs of frozen meat could be used as the crosspieces of a sled.

Wood, the most precious of materials, was not unknown. But since it was obtained only as driftwood, washed up from distant shores to the south, it was saved for special uses: a boat frame or a harpoon shaft. In view of such scarcity listeners could appreciate the command of magic in the story "The Girls Who Wished for Husbands." In this tale two brothers bury a piece of driftwood in damp sand, then dig it back up in sufficient quantity to make a boat.

The "boat" of folktales is always the *umiak* (OO-mee-ack), a skin-covered open boat about thirty feet long. When used for traveling, it was rowed by women, who sang as they rowed. Therefore the umiak was sometimes called the woman's boat. The long oars were held in place by rawhide oarlocks, called paddle strings in the stories. The umiak was also used by men alone, however, especially for hunting walrus and other large sea mammals.

For hunting seals, men typically used a smaller craft called the *kayak* (KIGH-yack), often referred to as the man's boat. The kayak was completely covered in skin, top and bottom, with only a small opening through which the single occupant could slip the lower half of his body. His special jacket, or half-jacket, was lashed to the rim of the opening so that the entire craft, even if overturned, was watertight.

The kayaker hunted with a long-shafted spear, or harpoon, tied to a cord that ended in an inflated sealskin "bladder float." A wounded animal, if it dived, could not carry off the harpoon, which remained attached to the float (see the story called "Kasiak"). Such gear was used only by adult men, but children played with toy kayaks and toy harpoons ("The Orphan Who Became Strong," "Little Bear").

The snow house, or igloo, was built only in winter, usually by two men working together. Blocks of hard snow were cut with slanted ends, so that they fit snugly when placed end to end. Laid in a spiral, the blocks formed a dome, to which a tunnel was attached as a weatherproof entrance.

More permanent houses, made of stone and sod, or whale ribs and sod, had the same form—dome and passageway—and were used year-round. The passageway was fitted with a door curtain at its inner end ("The Soul Wanderer") or, fancifully, in the case of a house inhabited by an evil sorceress, a curtain of bones ("The Adventures of Kivio"). Inside the dome was an earthen platform at the rear or along the sides, where people sat or slept. When visitors entered, they removed their outer clothing and placed it on a drying rack above the lamp.

Meat was usually kept outside in a small storehouse. Food could be prepared either indoors over the lamp or outdoors over a larger cooking fire.

People lived together in villages, especially in winter. In addition to the several family dwellings in the village, there might be a larger house where musical performances, story-telling, and dances were held (as mentioned in the story "Two Sisters and Their Caribou Husbands").

The supernatural

Every community had at least one gifted man or woman—the *angakok,* known in English as the shaman, medicine man, or medicine woman—whom other people looked to as a source of power. Shamans were relied upon to control the weather, find game animals, heal the sick, and ward off enemies. As part of their craft, they called out to helping spirits. Many had the ability to enter a semiconscious state in which the soul seemed to leave the body, flying to distant places in search of knowledge.

Inuit folktales are filled with shamans, both good and evil. In "The Lost Boys," a medicine woman magically protects the boys from enemies. In "The Woman Under the Sea," a little boy himself becomes an angakok and makes a soul flight to the bottom of the ocean in search of game. In the tale of Kivio, the hero barely escapes a cannibal woman who uses her shamanistic abilities to keep him from running away while she lights her cooking fire.

But everyone, shaman or not, felt in command of at least a small portion of supernatural power. This power was given at birth by a parent or other relative in the form of a charm that represented an animal helper.

In "Two Sisters and Their Caribou Husbands," the heroines have gull wing-tips as their charms, which give them gull power and therefore the ability to find fish. Similarly, the hero Kivio has the polar bear as his spirit helper, which magically comes to his aid when the cannibal shaman attempts to trap him.

Animals were thought to understand human needs and desires, and they themselves were regarded as humans in disguise. In folktales animals sometimes appear to be completely human, as in the case of the disagreeable husbands in the tale of the two sisters (the men are actually caribou). In "The Dancing Fox," by contrast, the fox has the form of an animal (though it can fold back the skin of its face to reveal the face of a human).

To call an animal spirit, or to seek supernatural aid in general, a person could use an incantation. The mere words were regarded as having irresistible power. Even to utter an idle wish could be dangerous, as we learn from the well-known Inuit tale "The Girls Who Wished for Husbands."

Another kind of magic, called divination, was widely used

to acquire hidden knowledge or to predict the future. In one form of divination, the user holds an object and asks yes-or-no questions. If the object suddenly seems to feel a little heavier, the answer is yes. An example is in the story called "Cannibal Village," where two brothers learn the whereabouts of the village by holding a seal line and asking it questions.

Still another form of magic depends upon similarity or common origin to set up a magnetic pull. In "Two Sisters and Their Caribou Husbands," caribou hairs are placed in a tub of water to attract the two husbands (who are caribou in disguise). The magic is doubly effective because in addition to the irresistible hairs, it is well known that caribou, when domesticated, are in the habit of drinking water from tubs or buckets. Therefore the caribou men cannot help but approach, and while they are drinking, the hunter who has prepared the tub and is lying in wait shoots them at close range.

Certain ideas about the supernatural may be counted as religious beliefs. For example, it was held to be true that a person's soul had a life of its own and could enter the bodies of animals or, in some cases, plants (see the story called "The Soul Wanderer"). It was even said that the soul could be contained in the person's name. Therefore a loved one who had died could, in a sense, be brought back to life by naming a newborn child after the deceased. This is why the bereaved parents in the story

"Kasiak" are overjoyed to hear that Kasiak has given their dead child's name to his own infant daughter.

In general it was believed that the dead went to live in a country beneath the sea. In "The Adventures of Kivio" this underworld realm is mentioned in a taunt: "Now you will go and taste the water in the country of the dead." In other words, prepare to die.

The underworld was also the home of the important deity Sea Woman, who had control of all the animals in the ocean. According to tradition, she had once been an ordinary human, whose fingers had been chopped off by her cruel father. The fingers swam off as sea mammals, while the woman herself sank to the ocean floor.

When food was scarce, shamans made soul flights to visit the woman in her undersea home, where they would help her by combing her tangled hair. (Having no fingers, she could not comb her own hair.) In exchange for the shamans' favor, she would release seals and other animals for hunters to catch. The story of how she saved one starving family in exactly this way is told in "The Woman Under the Sea."

Story sources

The richest collections of Inuit folktales are those made between 1860 and 1925 by three celebrated scientist-explorers,

Hinrich Rink, Franz Boas, and Knud Rasmussen. Rasmussen (1879-1933) was alone responsible for some five hundred stories, recorded in Greenland, Canada, and Alaska during the first quarter of the twentieth century. Danish on his father's side and Greenland Inuit on his mother's, he spoke Inuit from childhood and was able to communicate with native storytellers throughout the Arctic.

Rink (1819-1893) and Boas (1858-1942) were physical scientists who became attracted to the study of human culture early in their careers. Both had been geographers; in addition Rink had been a glaciologist, Boas a physicist. Turning to folklore, Rink produced a Greenlandic collection during the 1860s that included one hundred and fifty tales. Boas, who became the leading American anthropologist of his day, produced many volumes of native American folktales, including two Inuit collections from eastern Canada totaling one hundred and seventy-five stories.

The tales in the present book have been drawn principally from these three collectors—but with help from all other major works now available, including the collections of Holm, Thalbitzer, Edward Curtis, Diamond Jenness, and Robert Spencer. The method has been to select the strongest passages from all the available material. Thus the versions given here have been minutely edited, but not retold.

The same approach was used by both Rink and Boas, who could combine a half dozen or more texts obtained in the field in order to produce a single version of a particular well-known tale. The advantage is that the full range of incident, imagery, and sheer storytelling skill can be presented in a modest-sized volume. For those who wish to follow the process, a full accounting is provided in the Notes.

Over the years, folktale collectors have used a variety of spelling systems to represent Inuit words. The general rule, however, is that consonants have more or less the same sounds as in English; and vowels, though often long, as in Spanish or Italian (ah, eh, ee, oh, oo), are sometimes short, as in English bat, bet, and bit. Pronunciations for three familiar words, *Inuit, umiak,* and *kayak,* have been indicated above. In addition, the stories that follow include the names of five characters, Mako, Nepisinguak, Kasiak, Kinak, and Kivio, which may be pronounced MAH-koh, nay-pee-SING-oo-ack, KASS-ee-ack, KIN-ack, and KIV-ee-oh (not accurate pronunciations but very rough approximations for speakers of English).

Toward the future

Just as modern Europe, Africa, or Asia treasures the folktales of its not-so-distant past, the modern Inuit can look to their traditional stories as a precious cultural resource. Together with

Inuit sculptural and graphic art, the old stories, noted for their fascinating imagery and haunting realism, offer a contribution to world culture that becomes a source of pride as the Inuit join the international community–in a process that has quickened in recent decades.

Both culturally and politically the Inuit, since the 1970s, have moved toward greater prominence in the world at large. Between 1970 and 1980 important steps were taken to develop standard writing systems for Inuit people in Alaska, Canada, and Greenland so that publications in the Inuit language could be read throughout the Arctic.

At the same time a drive toward unity and self-rule began to gather strength as developments in the political sphere took shape in all three regions of Inuit territory. In Alaska a long-term campaign for land ownership produced the Alaska Native Claims Settlement Act of 1971, which in turn led to the establishment of conservation areas (protecting natural resources claimed by the Inuit) and to the transfer of school districts from state to local control.

In Canada, Inuit leaders in 1976 presented a formal claim to the Canadian government for ownership and user rights in three-quarters of a million square miles in the central Canadian Arctic, or about a fifth of the area of Canada. An accord was finally reached in 1991, designating an Inuit province to be called Nunavut ("our land").

In Greenland, the Home Rule Act of 1978 established the principle that taxation, social welfare, labor affairs, education, health services, and other areas would be transferred from Danish to Inuit control. Though still not independent of Denmark, Greenland is now known by the Inuit-language name Kalaallit Nunaat ("the land of the Greenlanders").

Meanwhile, a movement for Inuit unity across national boundaries has begun to show progress. In 1977 Inuit representatives from the three regions met in Barrow, Alaska, and formed an international organization known as the Inuit Circumpolar Conference (ICC). Additional Inuit communities in eastern Siberia, across the Bering Strait from Alaska, were under the control of the Soviet Union (now Russia), which kept them from joining. Since 1977 the ICC has continued to meet every three years either in Alaska, Canada, or Greenland, and since 1983 it has been a nongovernmental member of the United Nations.

Such important changes contrast sharply with the long-ago scenes brought to life by Inuit folk literature. Yet these recent developments and, in general, the new era of Inuit internationalism may be seen as complementing rather than contradicting the old stories, which, in themselves, are also a means of reaching out toward the rest of the world.

It is true that the elements of fantasy conjured up by the Inuit storyteller, not to mention the Arctic environment itself, are far removed from the world below. And it is undeniable that this remoteness helps give the stories their power.

Nevertheless, traditional Inuit literature should not be read merely for what is remote or different—that is, for glimpses of the northern lights or for perilous Arctic journeys or for strange giants in vast snowfields. It should be read for its vivid portrayal of an orphan who rises above his scornful neighbors, for little girls who regret their hasty wishes, for a resourceful woman who lives alone, or for the soul that yearns to have all experiences—in short, for its fresh insights into the basic themes that link this distinctive literature to the world community.

The Dancing Fox

ARCTIC FOLKTALES

The Adventures of Kivio

There was once a boy named Kivio who was greatly loved by his parents. His father, however, was often angry.

One day, when the father was out in his kayak hunting seals, the mother, who was tired of eating seal meat day after day, told the boy to take the other kayak and catch some fish for a change.

The boy protested, saying that his father had forbidden him to take the kayak. But the mother insisted, promising she would clean it and put it back in its place. "He'll never know," she said.

Then Kivio set out, carrying the kayak on his head. After a while he put it down in the water and paddled along the shore. He came to a river where there were fish and got out and walked along the riverbank with his net. When he had caught as many as he needed, he came back to the beach where he had landed and found to his great alarm that the tide had carried away the half-jacket belonging to the kayak.

As he paddled homeward, he became so worried that his father would be angry that he passed by his village and turned toward the open sea.

He paddled on. And when he looked behind him, the shore was almost out of sight. He kept on paddling, and when he looked around him again, he could no longer see land.

He was now far from shore. A storm came up, and the sea foamed and roared, driving him farther and farther away. He came to a place where the sea went bubbling around in a whirlpool.

"What can this be?" he thought.

"This is the Middle of the World," said a voice in the air.

He was nearly drawn into the whirlpool, yet he paddled on and escaped. Then he came in sight of two icebergs with a narrow passage between them that kept opening and closing. With great speed he pushed on and had just passed through when the icebergs closed together, bruising the stern-tip of his kayak.

At last he caught a glimpse of something dark, and before long he reached a great stretch of land rising up ahead of him. It was a land he did not know. He saw a house with smoke rising from the smoke hole, and he went ashore.

When he got to the house, he went in. At the far end of the passageway hung bones that rattled when they were touched. He drew them aside, they rattled, and the voice of an old woman came from within, saying, "Sit down.

"Sit down here," she said, stroking the place beside her invitingly with her hand.

The room was lit by two oil lamps, one on each side of the entrance. Over each of the lamps hung a piece of fat, from which oil dripped and fed the flames.

But the smoke that rose to the smoke hole came

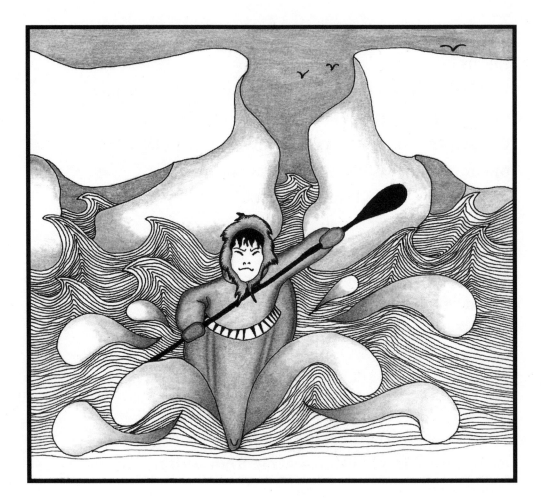

"With great speed
he pushed on and
had just passed
through when the
icebergs closed
together"

from the old woman's body. It was the smoke of her evil thoughts.

"Sit down and rest," she said. Then she saw that her visitor's boots were wet and offered to dry them for him. When she had put them on the drying rack, she went outside and built a fire. She acted as though she were going to prepare a meal, although there did not seem to be any meat in her house.

Looking around him, Kivio saw a great many skulls that he had not noticed before. One of these began to speak, saying, "The old woman eats all the strangers who enter her house."

Hearing this, Kivio wanted to run away. But he could not get hold of his boots. Whenever he reached out to take them, the drying rack shot into the air.

He had a huge white bear as his helping spirit, and it now came roaring up from under the floor of the house and pulled the boots down with its paw. Then without waiting to put the boots on, Kivio picked them up and ran out of the house to his kayak and paddled away.

The old woman rushed to the shore, shouting for him to come back. But Kivio skimmed over the waves like a falcon pursuing its prey and was lost to sight in less than a moment.

He paddled on. Again he turned toward the land and was just stepping ashore when, Oh heavens. What a surprise! A giant worm came rushing toward him. It was the old woman's helping spirit.

It called out to him, "Now you will go and taste the water in the country of the dead."

"I think you will go first," replied Kivio. Then he picked up his bow and reached for his arrows, and before he had even touched them he saw that the arrows were shaking. He breathed on them and made them alive. Then they flew from his bow. So fast did the arrows come flying that the worm, as the arrows hit him, looked just like a sparrow pecking the earth.

Then Kivio put out to sea again and traveled on. He came to a place where a heavy surf was pounding the beach. People on shore sighted him and said to themselves, "We will have some fun with him." These were the people who wore no clothes. In place of clothing they had feathers all over their bodies.

They called out to him: "Hello, little kayak! Approach!" Against his will, Kivio was drawn to shore, the rushing waters foaming around him.

When he hit the beach, some distance from the people who had called to him, he immediately turned his kayak keel upward and covered it over with crowberry plants and grass. He himself lay flat on the ground so they would not see him.

To catch his scent, they raised a wind. But Kivio raised a snowstorm, and they all froze.

Setting out again, he continued his journey. After a long time he saw a house on the shore. He landed and went up to it. In this house there were two women.

"I have just come from the feather-bodies," he said, "and now they are no more."

"Then thanks be to you!" they cried. "We, too, had a man in our house, but the feather-bodies finished him off. You must stay here with us. Tomorrow at low tide there will be fish."

The next morning Kivio was awakened by the roaring surf and saw the two women gliding out through the passageway. He jumped out of bed and threw on his jacket. By the time he reached the shore, the women had already harpooned several halibut.

The fish were kept afloat by bladders, but the wind was driving them out to sea. Kivio went after the fish with his kayak and brought them back, for which the women were grateful. "Thanks be to you!" they cried.

Kivio stayed with the women a long time. Then, remembering his old home, he asked the women to make him a pair of mittens, and they gladly did. He hid the mittens carefully, and the next day he complained of having lost them and asked for another pair. Another time he asked for another, and at a later time still another.

Now supplied with enough mittens for the long journey home, he slipped out of the house one morning before the sun had come up and soon was on his way. He traveled for many days without seeing anything.

Finally he came to a place where he heard a noise on the shore, but he did not see any houses. He heard someone crying, "Help me ashore!"

He landed and looked around. After a long search he found a mouse in a pool surrounded by steep rocks. The mouse was not able to get out. Kivio helped the mouse and went back to his kayak and paddled away.

He came to a great sea, which he crossed, and after a long time he came to a land that looked familiar to him, and he recognized his old country. He saw houses. They were his own village.

Suddenly he let out with a loud cry, so loud that the mountains echoed him. Kivio's old father and mother were sitting outside their house and heard it. They listened and listened and peered out over the sea.

The parents had been sitting on a stone by their house waiting for their son ever since he had been missed. So many years had they been waiting that even now you can see the hollows worn away in the stone where they sat.

"Listen," they said, "that sounds like Kivio's shout." And when they had recognized their son, they were so overwhelmed that their hearts broke and they both fell over and died with joy.

And so it is finished. That's all we know about Kivio.

Canada and Greenland

The Woman Under the Sea

There was a houseful of people at the edge of the sea. Winter was coming, and it was time to start filling the storehouses with meat.

Suddenly the weather turned bad with heavy gales. Snowdrifts came on earlier than usual, and there had hardly been a chance to catch any food.

Before the days began lengthening again, the sea

near the shore was completely frozen. As winter wore on, the bad weather continued, and most of the hunters stopped trying to find game. Inside the house people stayed in bed all day out of hunger and cold.

One morning when the elder people were all dozing on the platform and the children were playing on the floor, the oldest boy said, "Let's play calling up spirits."

Then the boy took off his jacket and hung it in front of the window. Meanwhile two of the younger children brought salt water and rinsed the floor to take off any foul odors that might keep the helping spirits away.

When all was ready the boy began to recite a charm:

Who is it
    that is coming to me?
The Soul of the Sea
    is coming to me.

The others now became frightened and started to run. But the moment they moved from their places the stone slabs of the floor rose into the air and rushed after them.

The boy would have run too, but he felt himself

sticking fast to the floor and could not get loose until he had ordered the other children to uncover the window. When the room became light again, he was able to get up. He made them all promise not to tell the elder people what he had done.

But when the elders woke up, the younger children forgot their promise and said, "We had fun today," and they told everything that had happened.

Hearing their story and desperate for any sign that might bring a change of luck, the elders insisted the boy try calling the spirits again. He was afraid. But with everyone urging him, he took off his boots and jacket and laid them aside. Then, reciting a charm, he called up two spirit-animals, and soon a bear and a walrus were roaring outside the house.

The bear took hold of the boy, carried him to the shore, and threw him to the walrus, who carried him farther, then hurled him back to the bear. In this manner the boy was thrown from walrus to bear, and from bear to walrus, farther and farther from his home country and downward into the sea.

He passed a slippery reef grown over with seaweed and beyond it a long slope covered with heather. Far

*"The bear took
hold of the boy...
and threw him
to the walrus"*

down, the land was level and a small river ran through it.

When he reached the edge of the river, the bear seized him for the last time and threw him down on the bank. As he lay there, his senses revived, and in front of him he could see a house.

He approached the entrance and saw that the passageway was as narrow as the edge of a knife. He entered nevertheless, and when he came to the inner room he found a tall woman sitting by her lamp, weeping, her face turned toward the wall.

Her hair was all loose and disheveled, and she cried, "What have you come for? What can you do to help me?"

The boy took hold of her tangled hair, combed it, and put it into a tuft on top of her head. Now the woman felt better. She became calm. Then she took down an eagle wing from a peg in the wall and stirred up the lamp to make it burn brightly.

For the first time the boy could see the wall behind the lamp. It was hung with skins like those used for boat covers. But although the lamp now burned steadily, he could see nothing in the deeper parts of the room. These remained in darkness.

Suddenly he heard the woman saying, "My guest

ought not to go alone. Let someone go with him as he leaves."

A moment later a little man with a very short nose emerged from the wall, and after him came a long line of the same kind of creatures, who began to file out through the passageway. When the last of them had vanished into the sea, they were all heard to cry kah-kah-kah sa-a-ah sa-a-ah—just like a flock of ice birds.

Soon other kinds followed, some with flat noses, others with crooked ones. But when they were getting too numerous, the woman cried, "Stop!"

While all this was happening, back at home on the floor of the house the boots and jacket the boy had left behind were shaking. The people of the house sat quietly on the platform, waiting in the darkness.

Meanwhile beneath the sea, still other kinds of little men were emerging from the shadows in the far corners of the Sea Woman's house. Some had large heads and beards. These too filed out through the passageway. As they left, they were barking like seals. When they had become too numerous the woman again cried, "Stop!"

The lamp was burning brighter than before. Now the boy could see that the passageway had become smooth and wide and that all the creatures who had passed through it had become game birds and seals. He found his way to the outside without difficulty, and on his way home he was again thrown back and forth by the bear and the walrus.

At last he entered his own house, where his relatives sat singing for him. As he approached, they cried, "Light the lamp!" But seeing that he was wounded all over from the teeth of the bear and the walrus, they put out the lamp again and continued singing.

The boy was barely breathing. But as his relatives sang, he revived a little. The next morning, when they looked out toward the sea they saw only ice. But within a few days, as the boy's wounds began to heal, a strong wind from the south set in.

A man who had gone out to look around came running back to say that the ice was breaking up. Moments later, ice birds were seen in great numbers.

Feeling stronger, the boy went outside, and the birds came and perched on him, crying kah-kah-kah sa-a-ah sa-a-ah. He touched them, and after he had captured just one, he caught them all and brought them inside.

His hungry relatives stretched out their lean hands,

and when all the people had tasted a little of the meat, one of the children said, "Ice birds are very nice, but what would make us eat still better?"

Then an old housemate pointed out a spot where partridges were sitting in the snow with their black beaks peeping forth. The boy went there at once and brought the birds back, cutting each one through at the joints, and in this way he shared the partridges equally among the people.

From then on he was constantly on the move, hunting on the land and also on the sea. When a shoal of seals came up, he threw his harpoon at the first one he saw and caught not only that one but the whole shoal at once, so that his harpoon line was full of seals.

When he returned with his catch, he said to the people, "If you have any need at all, you are each welcome to one of my seals."

The people helped themselves, and the old housemate said to him, "It is good that you give to others. Always act in this way, and the number of your captured animals will continue to increase."

And here it ends. I do not know any more.

Greenland

A Giant and Her Little Son

Long ago in the first days of the earth there lived a giant so tall she could stand with her right foot on one side of the bay and her left foot on the other side and wait for whales to pass beneath her. As soon as one came along, she stooped down and caught it in the hollow of her hand.

One day some people out in their boats had harpooned a whale and were trying to land it when the giant came by. She stooped over and lifted them up, boats, whale, and people. The whale made her smile, and she cried lil-lil-lil-lil-lil as it flopped its tail against the palm of her hand.

Then she put everything down on the beach and let the men keep the whale. But one of the whalers was a young boy who had come along with the men. She picked up the boy and said to him, "Little Legs! Will you be my son? I need a helper."

"Yes, if you will let me go bird hunting," he cried. There was no answer. The sound of his tiny voice, even though he shouted, was only a faint buzzing in the giant's huge ears.

Then he cried a little louder, "Can I go bird hunting?" And again he had to repeat it. This time he was shouting as hard as he could.

At last the giant heard him and said, "Why not?" and immediately started to call kee-kee-kee-kee-kee.

No sooner had she made the sound than the birds came flying over the water. The boy caught as many as he could carry, went ashore, flung them down, and came back for more. And from that day on he stayed with the giant.

*"she stooped
down and
caught it in
the hollow of
her hand"*

Another time he said to her, "I wish I could go hunting for narwhales."

"Why not?" she replied. Then she waded out into the sea and snorted like a narwhale, crying ho-ho-ho-ho-ho. When a narwhale appeared, the boy harpooned it, and they brought it ashore.

Winter came, and the giant lay down to sleep. But before she closed her eyes, she said to the boy, "Little Legs! Put this stone next to me. If you see a bear, hit me on the head with the stone until I wake up."

She had not been asleep very long when the boy saw a bear coming over the ice. He picked up the stone and hit the giant on the head. Then he pointed to the bear running toward them.

"Where is it?" she cried.

He pointed again.

"What, that little thing?" she said. "That's not a bear. It's just a fox." To her an ordinary bear was only a fox.

When it came close, she picked it up with one hand and gave it a good shake, and when she'd made a meal of it, she lay down to sleep once more.

But before she closed her eyes, she said to her little son, "Do you see those two bunches of seaweed? When the space between them is filled, *that* you may call a bear." To her they were nothing but bunches of seaweed, but to him they were islands in the sea with an enormous space between them. Then the giant went back to sleep.

At last, when winter was almost over, the boy saw something coming that filled the space between the two islands. Quickly he picked up the stone and hit it against the giant's head. She woke up. "Look," he shouted, "there's the bear!"

She jumped up. "Now *that* is a bear," she cried. Then she picked up the little boy and stuffed him into the top of one of her boots, and off they went.

The bear was so huge that it blocked out the sun. But the darkness did not last long. The giant picked up an iceberg and threw it, and the bear fell down in the water. Then she dragged the bear to shore, skinned it, and began cutting up the meat.

The boy worked beside her. But even with his help, it took so long to put the meat away that the willows growing over the hills had sprouted before they were finished. By the time they were done, spring had arrived.

And now, finally, they were well supplied with meat and could live easily. They had no house. They slept on the ground. The sky was their roof.

Canada and Greenland

The Lost Boys

Two boys were living with their parents in a house
at the edge of the sea. While the weather was warm,
the father caught fish and brought home furs and caribou meat. But summer was almost over, and soon the
family would have to leave for their winter village.

When the time came, the mother went to the drying
racks, took down the fish she had dried, and packed it

in the family's boat. Their furs, their caribou meat, and all their household belongings were put in the boat too.

When everything was loaded, the mother and father jumped ashore with the dogs and began to pull the boat along by a rope. The boys remained aboard to steer.

Suddenly the rope snapped, and the boat, with the two boys still in it, began drifting out to sea. The boys seized paddles and tried frantically to row toward the beach, but a brisk wind kept driving them seaward, while their poor parents, helpless, stood waving their arms on the shore.

In order to lighten the boat and make paddling easier, the boys threw all their belongings and most of their food overboard. But this only raised the boat higher out of the water, allowing the wind to push it more swiftly.

The older boy pretended he wasn't afraid. He comforted his little brother and told him not to cry. Night came, there was fog, and the wind blew them farther and farther away.

For days they were blown about. Often storms arose, threatening to swamp the boat. During a long period of foggy weather, they gave up all hope. But one night, while sleeping exhaustedly, they were awakened by the sound of the boat pounding on the bottom.

In the morning, when the fog cleared, the brothers found they had drifted to shore. Before them stretched a low, flat country, and close to the beach there was a strange village and many people. The younger boy wanted to go up to them at once, thinking they might be friendly. But his brother warned him, "No, we must be careful. These people are strangers."

They landed quietly and slipped across the beach without being noticed.

Close by were women cutting meat. Other people were lighting cooking fires. Men were dragging home seals, and there were drying racks hung with fish. The boys were hungry. But they did not dare to let themselves be seen.

Instead, they hid in the graveyard on the far side of the village. There among the grave posts they waited until it was dark. Then they slipped up to the houses and stole food. Next day they did the same, and the day after that.

The following day they found a small storehouse built on a raised platform. It was where the people of

"they hid in
the graveyard
on the far side of
the village"

the village kept their dried meat so that it would be safe from wild animals. When no one was looking, the boys stole some of the meat.

The next day they came back for more. And in this way they kept from starving. But at last, after many days, the villagers began to wonder who was stealing their food. They grew angry.

One day, when the people had gathered for a feast, the brothers overheard them talking about the stolen food. Perhaps birds or wild animals had discovered their storage place. No one knew for sure.

A medicine man was called. The people asked him to use his power to find out who the thieves might be. The man beat his drum and sang loudly, then announced: "I can learn nothing. There are no strange animals here, only humans. Humans must have stolen your food. Perhaps there are strangers nearby."

Then a second medicine man was called. His power was very great. He cried aloud: "Your food is being stolen by two persons. They are over there!"

Then the people noticed the brothers. But at first they could not believe that so much food had been stolen by two children. And so once again they called for help.

This time it was a medicine woman who came. She was old, and her power was the greatest of all. She ordered the people to go back to their houses. When they had left, she said to the boys, "Come! My spirit powers tell me I must take you with me. I will protect you and give you food."

The passageway to her home was well-lighted and crowded with dried foods and hunting equipment of all kinds. There she bathed the brothers and dressed them in fine clothing.

When they were bathed and clothed, she led them into the house itself, which was decorated with many strings of beads, and there were fine beds of caribou skins. The boys were each instructed to choose a bead, and these were strung with smaller beads and given to them to wear as headbands.

The brothers were kept inside until they were nearly grown. They became strong young men and learned athletic games, but they were not allowed to leave the house except late at night or when the villagers had gone away on a hunting trip.

No one knew that the old medicine woman had raised the two boys. But one day, when they disobeyed her and went outside, a medicine man saw them.

Soon a messenger appeared at the smoke hole. The old woman asked, "What do you want here?"

"The medicine man wants you and the two young men to come to the center of the village. You must all dress in your finest clothing, because you are about to die."

When they were ready, the messenger made the woman and the two brothers follow him to the shore, where a seal hunter stood poised with a harpoon. But just as the hunter was about to turn and kill them, the old woman used her magic, and the hunter was paralyzed. She would not let him move until the people came and brought her food and other gifts.

A second time the medicine man sent a messenger. And again a hunter stood poised, then turned to kill them. But he too was paralyzed by the old woman's power. Then again the people were forced to bring gifts.

And yet a third time the people tried to kill the boys. And again they were made to bring gifts, until at last there were many sealskin bags filled with food, clothing, and other valuables lying in a row beside the old woman's house.

In the fall of that year the medicine woman called the messenger to her and said, "These boys are now grown men, and it is time for them to visit their parents. They are the ones who stole food from the storehouse long ago. They must be allowed to go about the village now. You and the others who have tried to do us harm must build a large boat frame this winter. In the spring it must be provided with a skin cover and loaded with food and rich gifts of all kinds."

In the spring, when the boat was ready to be launched, the men pushed it into the water. Then they loaded all the food and gifts and raised the sail.

The two young men and the old woman got into the boat, taking the messenger along with them to be their pilot. A wind blew up, and soon they were on their way.

After a long journey, they reached the village where the boys' parents were living. The mother and father recognized their children at once and were filled with joy at the sight of them.

The old woman was joyful too, for she recognized the boys' father as her son. Then the boys knew that the old woman was their grandmother.

The family remained together for the rest of the

summer and throughout the long winter. When spring came again, the grandmother's boat was piled with food and many presents. Then, taking the pilot with her, she set sail and returned to her own country.

Alaska

Worms and Lice

It is said that our ancestors had no lice–lucky people. In the beginning there were no creatures of any kind that lived on people's bodies.

But then one day worms and lice decided to have a race to see who would be the first to reach human beings. Just as the race was about to begin, two lice were talking. They were husband and wife.

"Give me my mittens," said the husband.

"They're hanging on the post," said his wife. The couple lived in a caribou skin, and it was the hairs on the skin that the wife called posts.

"But let's stay here," said the wife. "Living on people would be too dangerous."

"Don't be afraid," said the husband. "Come. Let's go." And his wife handed him his mittens and off they went.

Then all the lice got into their umiak, and all the worms got into theirs. They rowed as fast as they could, racing to see which boat would be the first to get to the shore where people were living.

They chose the necks and the armholes of the people's jackets as their goal and kept shouting as they pulled at the oars:

Hurry on
    to the necks!
Hurry on
    to the armholes!

The lice were quicker. Their umiak pulled ahead.

*"Hurry on
to the necks!
Hurry on
to the armholes!"*

But their paddle strings broke, and the worms overtook them.

But then, when the worms were close to the shore, the same thing happened to them. Their paddle strings broke. And so the lice passed them by and got first to the necks and the armholes of the people's jackets.

"Never mind," shouted the worms. "People don't taste good anyway. We'd rather be the earth's lice!" Then all the worms came ashore and crawled into the ground.

Since that time, human beings have had lice. And worms have lived in the earth.

Canada and Greenland

The Girls Who
Wished for Husbands

It was a long time ago, and two girls were playing with bones on a beach. They were very young, and each of them still wore a child's hood. They were playing a game of mothers and fathers.

One of the girls picked up the shoulder bone of an eagle and said, "This one will be my husband."

The other girl pointed to a whale skull and said,

"This one will be *my* husband."

As they spoke, the bone of the eagle became a live eagle soaring in the air above them. At the same time the whale skull disappeared, and a live whale was seen spouting in the sea.

The eagle flew down and picked up the first girl by the tip of her hood and carried her off to be his wife. Then the whale came to shore and took the second girl out over the sea.

After that, the girl who had wished for an eagle husband lived on a ledge far up the side of a cliff. Every day the eagle would fly off to hunt and would bring back different kinds of small birds for food. The girl began to feel very homesick.

One time when the eagle was gone, a tiny woman appeared on the ledge where the girl was sitting and said to her, "Don't cry. Save the sinews from the wings of the little birds the eagle brings you, and I will show you how to get back to your old home again."

From then on the girl constantly urged the eagle to go hunting so she would have plenty of sinew to store up. While he was away, the tiny woman showed her how to spin out the sinew to make rope. The little woman was a spider.

*"the tiny woman
showed her how
to spin out the sinew
to make rope"*

One day the girl tried the length of the rope and found that it reached all the way to the bottom of the cliff. When the eagle returned, she asked him to bring her up a big stone. "I'll use it as my seat," she declared.

But the next day when the eagle was off hunting, she tied one end of the line to the stone and went sliding down to the ground.

Just as she was running toward her home, the eagle returned to the cliff. Seeing that his wife had escaped, he threw away his catch and flew to the beach where he had first seen her.

The girl got home to her parents with no time to spare. And now the eagle was soaring above the house, beating its wings. The girl's brother came out and said, "If you want to show that you have married into our family, spread your wings and hold them out wide."

As the eagle held out its wings, the brother shot it full of arrows, and when it fell to the ground it was changed once again into a bone.

Now, the other girl who had been taken away was living together with the whale in his enormous house on an island far from the shore. Afraid of losing her, the whale would not let her out of his sight for even a moment. And in no time at all she, too, began to feel homesick.

Unnoticed by the whale, the girl was visited by a tiny woman, who taught her to save sinew and spin rope. The one who came to her was the spider woman, and when at last the girl had made a long length of rope, she said to her husband, "You may tie me to this and hold the other end. That way I can go out when I need to, and you won't have to worry about losing me."

By this time the girl's two older brothers were beginning to miss their sister very much. Searching the beach, they found a piece of driftwood, which they buried in the damp sand. After a while, when they dug it up again, it had increased greatly. It was enough for the framework of a boat.

Setting to work immediately, they made a swift-sailing umiak. And when they had finished it and got it into the water, they said, "Now let us see how fast it can go."

They found a long-tailed duck that had a nest close by and got it to fly beside them. They tried to outdistance it by rowing. But when it flew past them, they cried, "This will not do. The whale would catch us at once."

And so they took the boat apart and used the pieces to build a new one. Again they put it into the water and let the bird race with them. This time they kept side by side with the duck, and as they came near the island, the bird fell behind them.

Just then their sister was handing the end of the rope to the whale and was going outside through the passageway. Seeing her two brothers, she loosened the rope and twisted it around a stone. Already the whale was pulling on the other end. But she ran quickly to the umiak, and as soon as she had jumped in, her brothers turned the boat around and began rowing back to shore.

Within moments the whale came out through the passageway and rolled down to the sea. The umiak was swift, but the whale soon caught up with it.

"Throw out your hairband," cried the brothers. And hardly had their sister thrown out her hairband than the sea foamed up, and the whale stopped. But in a short while it came after them again.

"Throw out your mitten," they cried. And again the sea foamed up, and the whale stopped. But before long it had overtaken them yet again.

"Throw out your other mitten," they cried.

And at that moment the sea was lashed into foam. But by now the umiak had come to shore. When the whale tried to follow, it was cast up on the beach, and just in that instant it was changed into the sun-bleached skull it had been before. Then the girl ran up the beach and was home at last.

It was the spider woman who had made it possible for those two girls to escape. Thanks to her, both were returned safely to their brothers and their parents.

And that's why today we don't kill spiders–they're so helpful.

Alaska, Canada, and Greenland

The Orphan Who Became Strong

There was once an orphan who lived with his grandmother, and they had no one to care for them. They were not even allowed in the main room of the house but had to stay in the passageway, where they tried to warm themselves by lying close to the dogs.

The little boy was small and could do no work. He could only play games. If the children who played with him grew tired, then others took their places. That was the way with him. He played from morning until evening.

At night when he returned to the house, the people treated him badly. Only a few took pity on him. When the men and the women went in and out, they stepped on his feet, and they used his hair for wiping their hands.

Sometimes kind people would give him food. But usually all he could get was walrus skin thrown to the dogs, and because he had no knife to cut it with he had to tear it with his teeth. When they saw him chewing on a piece of hide, there would always be someone who would say, "Oh, look! He must have gotten a new tooth!"

They would make fun of him and rip his shirt. Then he would cry and turn to his grandmother, and she would quiet him and mend the shirt. Day after day they ripped his clothes, and his grandmother would mend them, until finally the old woman had used up all her thread. Then she went to the people and said, "Someone would beg clothes for her grandchild."

"Let children go naked," they replied, and again they laughed and made fun of the little boy.

No one thought this boy could ever be anything.

Other children, who were younger, grew up and began to catch seals. But the old woman's grandchild did not grow. He did not change in the least, no more than a doll changes. At times, it is true, his grandmother spoke of what they should do to make him grow a little, but it could not be done. He never changed at all.

When the time of ripe berries came, he went out in the middle of the night before the other children were awake. But as soon as they saw him coming home, they ran up to him and pushed him down as easily as if he had been an empty skin. All the berries he had picked were spilled on the ground.

One day his grandmother said to him, "Tomorrow you must go out into the great hills. Tell no one. And when you reach the place where the two ravines running north lie straight before you, cry out, 'Let the Master of Strength come!'"

The next day the boy went off by himself. When he reached the mountains he called out:

Master of Strength,
   come.
Master of Strength,
   come to me.

And hardly had he spoken the words than a great dog appeared. He would have run away, but he could not move from the spot. At last the dog came up to him, and twisting its tail around his body, threw him down. Unable to get up, he kept hearing a rattling sound. When he looked to see what was there, he saw toy kayaks all over the ground. They had been shaken out of his body.

Again the dog wrapped its tail around him. He felt himself spinning. And just as before, something fell rattling all over the ground. When he looked, there were toy harpoons.

A third time the dog twisted its tail, and the rattling noise was heard. The boy looked again and saw little dolls scattered in every direction.

When there was nothing more to come, the great dog turned to him and said, "It is on account of all these little toys that you could not grow. And because of them, you had no strength." Then the dog left him.

On his way home he came to a dried-up lake, and in the middle of it lay a huge stone half-buried in the clay.

He went up to the stone and lifted it so easily that nothing was heard except one sound when the clay said, "Thup!"

*"The boy looked
again and saw
little dolls
scattered in
every direction"*

Suddenly he felt much stronger, and he ran home kicking stones right and left.

That night he again lay down to sleep among the dogs. But his grandmother could see his excitement. "You must say nothing about this to anyone," she said.

By morning he had already begun to grow taller. When his grandmother saw what had happened, she covered him over so that no one coming into the house would notice. The day was well along when a cry came through the window, "Come out and play."

His grandmother answered for him, "I'm sorry. He's sick." When this was heard, there was laughter, and they all went away.

Every day he grew in height. But his grandmother kept him covered. Every day the others would tell him to come out, and the old woman would always answer, "He's getting worse and worse." Only his head was peeping out of the covers. "He's scarcely able to breathe," she would say, and the children would mock him and laugh.

One day, after winter had set in and the sea had become frozen, three bears came over the sea ice, close to the village. Men went out to hunt them, but seeing how big they were, they were afraid. They ran back to the house, crying, "Where is the little boy? We'll give him to the bears to feed on. We can use him as bait."

They called him again and again, and finally he answered, "Here is the little boy!" Then he came out from the passageway, singing:

While I slept,
    I had the dogs for my blanket.
While I slept,
    you stepped on my hands.

At first they did not recognize him. He had become tall and strong. When they realized who he was, they were amazed. Then he sprang to the edge of the ice, and the hard snow flew up around him as he ran.

Coming directly to the bears, he kicked them aside, then picked them up by the legs, one by one, and struck them on the ground as though he were knocking snow out of clothing.

"This one is for my jacket," he cried. "This one is for my trousers. This one is for my boots." Then he dragged the three bears to the village and called to the people to come get their share of the meat—all except those who had tormented him.

Turning to each in turn, he gave them a look, and they all leaped into the air as ravens. Then he followed them with his eyes as they flew toward the sloping hills, and with that they were quickly out of sight.

After the meat had been cut up and the cooking fire had been started, people picked up the skins and brought them into the house, saying, "This one is for his jacket. This one is for his trousers. This one is for his boots."

When the people had eaten, the boy turned to his grandmother and gave her the best seat in the house.

From that time on he became a mighty hunter and a great man among his neighbors. When he hunted caribou, he would come back to the village, calling, "Grandmother, I have got you skins to lie upon." And the people would see him coming, handsome to look at and in handsome clothing. His grandmother had made him a new suit and new boots with soles of many thicknesses.

In the pride of his heart he roamed all over the country to show off his strength. He became famous at all the winter settlements, and in many places the marks of his great deeds are still shown. That is what we have heard tell.

Alaska, Canada, and Greenland

Two Sisters and Their Caribou Husbands

Two sisters lived with their older brother, and they lived happily. They had their winter quarters at the edge of a bay. When they went out hunting, the brother took his kayak, and the sisters ran along the beach. They watched each other, and the three of them always returned home at the same time.

One day when the sea was frozen, the sisters walked

over the ice by themselves. They were on their way to the outer islands to gather roots. Suddenly an east wind overtook them. The ice broke up, and they were carried far out to sea in very bad weather.

After a while the sky became clear, and they came in sight of high land. They drifted toward it and came to shore safely. They were almost fainting from hunger. Looking behind them, they saw that the ice floe that had been carrying them had turned to foam.

Each of them had the wing-tip of a gull for a charm. They now wandered across the beach and came to a little bay into which a river emptied. "There must be salmon here," said the older sister, "or there would not be so many gulls." Then, holding her charm, she said these words:

Dweller of the sea.
Let it rise up.
Its breath
I wish to hear.

Instantly a salmon appeared. They made a fire by rubbing pieces of wood together and put the fish on a stone to fry.

It was now low tide. The beach was turning dry, and all along the shore there were seals. They caught as many as they needed.

One day, having made their camp at this place, they noticed two men in kayaks, out seal hunting. Seeing the two sisters, the men cried, "Well, whoever gets ashore first will marry the prettier of the two."

With that they took to their paddles, and the first man to reach the shore touched the older sister, the other man taking the younger. Completely forgetting their hunt, they hurried home to get an umiak. Before long they returned. Then they put the two sisters into the umiak and brought them to their house. There they all lived happily for some time.

After a while each of the sisters had a daughter, and as they walked about with their little babies in their arms, they hummed to them and told them of their native land and of their old home on the other side of the sea. But the two men had fallen silent.

The husband of the older sister was thinking, "Why doesn't my wife have a son?" He would rub his hair next to his temples upward so that his hair stuck straight up. Finally he said to his wife, "What is the matter with you that you don't give me a son?"

Meanwhile the husband of the younger sister found a large tree that had been thrown to shore. He dragged it up the beach and carefully balanced it against the house in such a way that if he touched it slightly it would come down through the roof. Then he threatened the younger sister that if she had a daughter next time, he would cause the tree to crush the house and everyone in it.

One day, when the two sisters happened to be all by themselves, they began to cry. It was difficult to keep the tears back. Then, having wept away their sorrow, they made a plan.

"We'll pack our clothes," said the older sister, "and as soon as the ice forms, we'll return to our old home. But don't let them suspect anything."

Ice soon covered the sea. The time for hunting seals came to an end, and the men, having nothing else to do, went out visiting at a large house close by, where they enjoyed themselves dancing.

One night when there was to be a dance, and all the other women had gone to look on, the sisters put their infants in their jacket hoods and walked up and down outside, lulling them to sleep.

When they heard singing from within the big

*"they hastened
away with
their children
in their hoods"*

house, they hastened away with their children in their hoods, carrying their extra clothes. All night long they walked on the ice.

At daybreak they reached land and recognized a place where they had once had a winter camp. They went on a little farther and look! There was their own little house, just as they had left it.

Their brother was astonished to see them entering the passageway and immediately questioned them about the land across the sea. "In that country," they said, "there *is* something for a hunter."

"Well then, let me hear about it," he said. And they told him of salmon they had caught, seals they had found on the dry beach, and caribou that were to be hunted inland.

"I really must try that country," he said. "We will go in spring after the seals appear."

When the days had lengthened, the brother took down his umiak, and on its side he drew two charms, a duck and a salmon. As soon as all was ready, he went to the top of a hill to feel the weather, and as not a breath of wind was stirring, he came back to the house, saying, "It is calm. Let us be off."

Then they pushed away from the shore, the sisters

carrying their infants in their jacket hoods. Traveling westward, they entirely lost sight of their own country.

When they wished for speed, the umiak raised itself over the water by the force of its charms and sailed along as swiftly as a duck flies. When they wished for slower speed, it moved through the waves like a swimming salmon.

Suddenly the brother shouted, "I see land rising up!" As they came closer, the sisters recognized the bay where they had come ashore the year before. At the same time, they recognized their former husbands. The angry husbands had seen them approaching and were now running out to attack them.

Before he had left home, however, the brother had packed a pair of caribou stockings taken from the grave of an ancestor. He now filled a tub with fresh water and added some dust mixed with hairs from the stockings. Touching the shore, he set the tub on a rock where the attackers would have to pass.

When the two men came to the tub, they could not resist taking a drink. As each took a sip, he was changed into a caribou. Then the brother, who was waiting close by, shot the two caribou, and they rolled into the sea.

Soon afterward the companions of the caribou men came running up. Like the two before them, all took a drink from the tub of fresh water, became caribou, and were shot. And as they fell, they rolled into the sea.

For a while the brother and the two sisters stayed in the far country. They fished for salmon and dried them. They prepared caribou hides. Then they caught seals, skinned them, and prepared more hides. After filling the umiak with these and many other valuables, they took to the water and again reached their old home.

All that they had gotten they stored in chests. And from that time on, whenever the chests needed to be opened, they merely touched them and the covers unlocked of themselves, because of the great quantity of clothes they contained.

They built a large house with three windows. They had plenty to eat. They stayed rich and never went hungry.

This story we have from the days of our ancestors. And here it ends.

Greenland

The Land of the Birds

Yes, once upon a time–the usual story–there was a young man who needed a wife. The old people used to tell it. We heard it this way:

A young hunter had wandered far inland. Suddenly he heard the voices of women. He searched everywhere but could find nothing. At last he came in sight of a small lake, and there in the distance he saw a flock of geese swimming.

On the shore were many pairs of boots, all beautifully made. Without making a sound he crept nearer and stole the boots. After a while, the birds came out of the water and, finding the boots gone, became alarmed and flew away.

Only one of the flock remained behind, crying, "I want my boots, I want my boots."

Then the young man came out from his hiding place and asked, "Will you be my wife?"

She did not reply but kept looking for her boots. Again he asked her, "Will you be my wife?"

At last she said, "Yes, I will be your wife. But first you must give me my boots." He gave her the boots, and when she had put them on she was changed into a woman.

Then he brought her to his house, and there they lived as husband and wife. After a while they had a son.

When the little boy was growing, his mother would lead him down to a lake not far from the house. At the lakeshore she showed him how to eat grass mixed with sand and pebbles. She taught him never to eat meat.

One day when the husband had helped kill a whale

and was busy cutting it up, he noticed that his wife stood by, doing nothing. He called to her and asked her to help with the work. "My food is not from the sea," she replied. "My food is from the land."

Sometimes she would take her son out walking, and together they would pick up feathers. She would say to him, "My son, the birds are your relatives."

One autumn, when the wild geese were flying away, she took the feathers they had collected and stuck them between her son's fingers and over his arms and shoulders. When she had done the same to herself, the two of them rose into the air as geese.

They flew to a nearby lake where the boy's father was fishing for salmon. They circled over him, and the mother cried, "We are going home to our own people." And with that they were gone.

Then the husband left his salmon fishing and followed his wife and child to the land of the birds, traveling far beyond the horizon.

He started off at a run, crossing over hills in the direction they had flown. He traveled on and on, and after a long while he saw two wolves directly in front of him, one on each side of the path. He tried to go around, but every time he took a step sideways, the

"*she took the feathers
they had collected
and stuck them
between her son's
fingers and over his
arms and shoulders*"

wolves were in his way. Then he rushed between them and came through safely.

He ran on. Then he came to a cooking pot that stood on the ground all bubbling and boiling, talking to itself: po-po-po-po-po. It was full of meat, and it tried to tempt him, and every time he put his foot down to go around it, it was in front of him.

Then he jumped into the pot, stepped on the pieces of meat, and crossed over.

Traveling on, he came to two large rocks that opened and closed. He went to one side, then to the other, trying to go around them. But they were always there. He was afraid to go between them, but then, watching his chance, just as they opened he slipped through.

After many days he came to a river that emptied into a large lake. On the bank of the river he saw a man chopping chips from a piece of wood. As the chips fell, the man polished them neatly and they were changed into salmon, becoming so slippery that they glided from his hands into the river and on into the lake. The name of this man was Little Salmon.

The husband of the goose wife said to Little

Salmon, "My wife has left me. Haven't you seen her coming this way?"

Little Salmon replied, "Do you see that island far off in the lake? There she lives now."

"But I don't know how to reach her."

Then Little Salmon gave him the backbone of a fish and said, "Close your eyes. The backbone will turn into a kayak and carry you safely to the island. But don't peek, or the boat will turn over."

He promised to obey, and when he had closed his eyes, the backbone became a kayak. Off he went across the lake. But he could hear no splashing of water and was afraid that the boat was not really moving. He opened his eyes just a little, and scarcely had he taken a peek than the kayak began to swing violently, and he felt it becoming a backbone again.

He quickly shut his eyes. The boat went steadily on, and in a short time he landed on the island.

Not far from the beach was a village, and in front of one of the houses his little son was playing. When the boy saw his father, he ran to his mother, crying, "Father is here!"

His mother answered, "Your father is far away and can never find us."

But the boy called again, "Father is here! He is coming to our house."

"Tell him to come in," said the mother.

Then the father went in. But when he tried to sit down beside his wife, she flew off and settled in the other part of the house.

The man went after her and sat down again beside his wife. But now she flew to the spot where she had been sitting at first. The man moved over to her once again, but this time he put his finger to his lips and touched her with it before sitting down. Then she stayed where she was and did not fly away from him ever again.

And so the man found his way to his wife and his son. And from that time on he lived in the land of the birds.

And yes, that's the end of this story.

Alaska, Canada, and Greenland

Kasiak

There was once a man whose name was Kasiak. Some called him the Great Liar. "Oh! My husband is so great in his lies!" his wife would say, and she would slap his cheeks until his eyes popped out just a little. She did this because he told so many lies.

People say that Kasiak could never sleep well at night, and being sleepless, he kept everyone else awake when they had to go hunting the next day. He himself, however, never caught anything.

When he came home empty-handed, his wife would scold him. One night she scolded him worse than usual, and when she looked for him the next morning he had disappeared. All day long she was restless. She was fidgety, running in and out, looking for him, hoping he might be bringing something.

At last she saw a tiny spot in the distance. "A kayak!" she cried.

It was Kasiak. He had tied a stone to his harpoon line, telling the others, "A walrus has just gone down with my bladder floats! Haul it up while I row to shore and tell the news!" And as soon as a shout could reach the land, he called out, "A lucky hit! I've struck a walrus. The others are bringing it in."

His wife jumped up in such a hurry she broke the handle of her knife. But she didn't mind. "Now I can get a walrus-tooth handle," she said, "and a new hook for my kettle."

When Kasiak got to shore, he went inside to rest while the others hauled in the meat they had brought. Nothing could be seen of Kasiak—only his heels sticking out over the edge of the sleeping platform.

The women ran down to the beach with the cry: "Kasiak has struck a walrus!" They repeated it as each of the kayaks pulled up. But when the last man had come ashore, he said to them, "Do not believe it. Here are Kasiak's bladder floats. They were tied to a stone, and the knot worked loose."

"What am I hearing?" cried Kasiak's wife, and she ran to her husband, saying, "Oh, Kasiak, you've lied again."

"Hrrrrrrr," he said, to shoo her away.

Another day, when he was out kayaking along the coast, he noticed some loose pieces of ice on a sandy beach. Two women gathering berries were watching as he rowed to shore. They saw him fill his kayak with bits of the ice, and after stuffing more ice into his jacket, he turned toward home.

As soon as he saw his wife, he started to wail, "Poor me! An iceberg broke apart and fell on top of me!"

"Poor you!" she cried, and she ran to get him some dry clothes. As the last of the ice came tumbling out of his jacket, he groaned and said, "What a close call!"

Throughout the day his wife repeated the tale of her husband's narrow escape. But when the two women who had been berrying came back to the village and heard the story, they said, "Isn't this the one we saw stuffing his clothes with ice?"

"Oh, Kasiak, you've lied again," said his wife.

"Hrrrrrrr," he said, to shoo her away.

Another day, he went visiting in his kayak and came to the village where his father-in-law lived. When he entered the house it was dark inside because there was no blubber to burn in the lamps, and the father-in-law's little son was crying.

"What's the matter with him?" asked Kasiak.

"He's hungry, as usual," said the mother. "We have no meat."

Kasiak cleared his throat loudly and said, "We're having a hard time ourselves. Yesterday the women and I had our hands full with all the seals and walruses that had been caught. I've got both my storehouses choked full of them. And now my arms are sore from so much work."

"Oh!" exclaimed the father-in-law. "Who would ever have thought that poor Kasiak would turn out to be such a rich man!" And he began to cry with emotion. Kasiak pretended to cry with him.

When he left, he told his father-in-law to let the little boy go with him in order to bring back some food. "There's plenty of meat at my place," he said.

When they reached home, Kasiak made a snare from a piece of string, took some scraps of frizzled blubber from his wife's lamp, and threw these out as bait to catch ravens.

Suddenly he cried, "Two! No, wait. The other one got away." He ran out and brought back one raven, and his wife skinned it and boiled it. After that, the poor little brother-in-law, still hungry, had to look to the other villagers for food.

Then Kasiak's wife scolded her husband: "Oh, Kasiak, you've lied again."

"Hrrrrrrrr," he said, to shoo her away.

Another day, he heard that a married couple in a village down the coast had lost their child. Immediately he went on a visit. When he got to the village, he entered the house, and there sat the couple, mourning. Kasiak went over to the other people of the house and asked in a low whisper, "What's the trouble?"

"They're mourning," he was told.

"What for?" he asked.

"Suddenly he cried, 'Two! No, wait. The other one got away'"

"They've lost a child. Their little daughter died the other day."

"What was her name?"

"Nepisanguak," they said.

Then Kasiak cleared his throat and announced in a loud voice, "We've just got a little daughter at home. We've named her Nepisanguak."

At this, the mourning parents and all their relatives cried, "Thanks be to you! Thanks that you have called her by that name!" And they began to weep. Kasiak pretended to weep with them, covering his face with his fingers.

Then they feasted him with rich things to eat. Kasiak continued, "Our little daughter cannot speak plainly yet. She only says 'beads.'"

"Beads!" they cried. "Here, take these." And when he left, his kayak was loaded with beads and other gifts—china plates, seal paws, and an iron pot.

When he got home he said to his wife, "What a dreadful accident! A shipwreck! And all these things tossed about on the ice!"

His wife took one look at the iron pot and ran into the house to give her old cracked pot a smash. She threw away the shoulder blades they had been using for plates. Then she sewed the beads on her jacket and walked back and forth to make the beads rattle.

The next day a great many kayaks were announced. Kasiak instantly jumped up on the sleeping platform and got back as far as he could. Only his heels were seen sticking out over the edge.

As soon as the kayakers put in to shore, they called out, "Tell Kasiak to come down and help carry these extra gifts we've brought for his little daughter."

But the only reply was, "Kasiak has no daughter. His wife is childless."

At this news they quickly got up to Kasiak's house and took back the pot and all the other gifts they'd given him the day before. They cut the beads off his wife's jacket, and when they had left, she scolded him worse than ever, slapping his cheeks and pinching him.

"Hrrrrrrrr," he said, and they kept on scolding and pinching each other until at last they fell asleep, exhausted.

All this we have heard tell of Kasiak. And so it ends.

Canada and Greenland

The Woman Who Lived by Herself

There was once a married couple whose only child died, and the husband in his grief was unable to say a word. The reason was that his sadness had turned to anger, and it could not get out of his body. The drum song says:

As I do not seem to be angry,

It is happening inside me.

If I were just ordinarily angry,

It would happen outside me.

Becoming so angry he was dangerous.

Then one day without warning he went away in the umiak, leaving his wife behind. He took the other members of his household with him, and while they were rowing, one of the women in the boat said, "Why are you going away and leaving your wife?" But he pretended not to hear.

The woman who had been left behind was soon to have another child. She now went inland through a large valley that led north. She continued in that direction until she caught sight of the sea.

At the water's edge there was a little hill, which she thought must be a gull mound. But when she came closer, she saw that it was a stranded whale, left high and dry by the tide. And on top of the whale a gull was perched, busily pecking away at the hide.

She went up to the whale, cut it in pieces, and walked inland, carrying heavy loads of meat.

At a distance from the sea she built a house, making a solid frame of whale ribs and filling the spaces in between with sod and turf. Using whale gut, she made windows.

With a good house to live in, she settled herself and waited. In time she gave birth to a daughter.

As the little girl began to grow, she had many dolls to play with. The dolls were made by her mother, using seal paws.

Along the beach the mother would sometimes find a seal carcass that had drifted to shore. She would then have blubber to burn for heat and light, and she would also have meat. Near the house was a salmon creek, and this also provided food.

When winter set in, she shoveled snow over the house to make it warm. Then foxes came down from the hills to eat what was left of the whale. The woman caught them in snares she had made from the whale's sinews.

Once when she awoke from sleep, she saw foxes eating the meat she'd stored for the winter. These also she caught with snares, and she used the skins for sleeping rugs for her bed. Soon she had enough even to hang on the walls.

"Along the beach
the mother would
sometimes find a
seal carcass"

She had no needles and no thread, but she used sinews to fasten the skins together, making wall coverings and every kind of clothing—jacket, shirt, trousers, and stockings.

One day when spring had come and she was preparing a new window skin, her daughter knocked down one of her dolls and cried, "My doll is beginning to run!"

Her mother scolded her, "Don't say that. Just play with your dolls."

The child repeated, "One of my dolls is running!"

A few days later the child exclaimed, "Mother, my doll can speak! It says my father is coming tomorrow."

"You have no father. Didn't you know?"

But the little girl answered, "The doll says, 'When the dark has come and gone and there's light again, your father will be here.'"

They lay down to sleep. When it became light, they heard a rattling outside. The mother looked through the window and saw a man driving up in a sled.

The man entered the house, and the woman recognized her husband. "How did you manage to catch all the foxes?" he asked. "These skins completely cover the walls!"

"I caught them with snares," she answered. Then she told him how she had found a whale.

He slept there that night, and the next day he wanted to take his wife home with him on the sled. But she would not go. The husband went off again by himself, and the mother and daughter lived on through the summer and another winter.

When spring came again, they went to the place where the husband was living, and at last, when summer arrived, the woman took the man to be her husband just as before, and they lived together again for a long while.

After her husband's death, the woman remained in that place alone with her daughter and was able to catch seals and other animals. She even caught caribou. She could do anything she set her mind on!

Now that's the story.

Greenland

Cannibal Village

A family had three children. The oldest was a daughter, who had married a man from far away in the south when her two brothers were still small. As the boys grew up, they knew nothing of their sister, because their father deliberately never mentioned her. But when they were quite grown and had begun to catch seals, their mother said to them one day, "I think you don't even know that you have a sister!"

Hearing these words, the older boy said, "Make some warm clothes for me and my brother. We are going to find our sister." At the same time he began to make a sled. Then, when autumn came and the snow fell, so that they could drive over the sea ice, the two brothers set off for the south.

Before they left, their mother said, "You'll recognize your sister by her hair, which, strange to say, is quite white on one side."

After traveling for a long while, they reached the high mountains in the south and began to watch the base of the slopes for some sign of houses. Finally the older brother said, "When people live at the foot of a mountain, ravens are sure to be soaring in the air above."

Soon they sighted a craggy hill, and above it a great many ravens were flying. The brothers now turned away from the frozen sea and came toward the shore.

Wishing to know if their sister's house was nearby, they made a spell by pulling on a seal line. They asked the line a question, and when the answer was yes the line would become heavier. But if the answer was no, the line would become lighter.

The older brother asked, "Is my sister nearby?" The line became a little heavier, and they traveled on. Again: "Is she nearby?" The line became very heavy.

At that moment the sled dogs picked up a scent, and just as darkness was falling they came in sight of houses built one above the other on the mountainside. There were so many that the lights in the windows looked like torches.

"Wait here," said the older brother. "I am going to look in at all the windows, beginning with the uppermost." And when he had reached the window of the highest house, he looked in through a hole in the window skin and saw a woman all white on one side of her head.

Then he went and got his brother, and the two boys entered the house and greeted their sister. Beside her sat her husband, a great man broad of build, who now reached up to take something from the drying frame. But his wife said, "Wait, these are my dear younger brothers."

When her husband heard this, he put back the knife he had been reaching for. From then on he acted like a good brother-in-law. It was as if he had just awakened,

*"the sled dogs
picked up a scent"*

so kindly did he behave toward his wife's brothers. He told his wife to prepare a meal.

Before going out to the storehouse, the wife put on her boots, assisted by her two little children. And after a while a large tub of berries mixed with blubber was set before the two brothers.

The visitors were beginning to feel at ease and were just about to help themselves when they caught sight of a human hand floating among the berries. The little children saw it at the same moment. "Oh, Mother," they both cried, "please let us have some too!"

At this the two brothers rose from their seats, and the younger said to the older, "We visit too few houses. Let us go out and see other people."

So they went down to the lowest house, which lay farthest to the south. It was a long house, filled to the middle with young girls, and on the opposite side were many people young and old.

Next to the window frame sat a man mending his hunting gear. He rose up at once and greeted the two brothers. From close behind him they could hear a loud smacking of lips, and from across the room came the sound of the girls greedily rattling their knives.

The brothers sat next to a kindly woman who whispered to them, "If they try to eat your feet, cover them up with your hands." But even as she spoke, her nostrils twitched at the smell of their flesh.

"We visit too few houses," said the younger brother. "Yes," said the older boy. "Let us go see other people."

Quickly they rose from their seats and went out through the passageway. By now the entire village knew that strangers had arrived, and from every direction people could be heard howling like dogs when they know their meal is ready.

Returning to their sister's house, the brothers met their sister's husband at the door. "We had thought to stay here the whole winter," they said, "but now we must leave right away."

"Well, you know where we live," replied the brother-in-law. "Do come back and visit your sister." Then he said to his children, "Be good to your mother's brothers. Go out and cut all the lashings of our neighbors' sleds, and don't make any noise."

The children went out immediately, and when they came back they were asked, "Did you do as I told you? Did you cut them all?"

"Yes," they answered. "We did."

But they had forgotten one of them.

Now the two brothers ran to their own sled, and just as they were off they heard the nearest neighbor call to his dog, "Hype-sype-sype-sype-sype, there's a stranger in sight, isn't there, Long Hair?" The dog rushed to the man's sled.

In a moment, people everywhere were running to their sleds with cries of "Look! They're getting away!" Then the entire village set to work so busily that one might have thought it the flickering of the northern lights.

But the brothers were already halfway to the shore. Looking over their shoulders, they could see that those who were trying to follow stuck fast as soon as they started. With the lashings all cut, their sleds fell to pieces. All but one.

As the brothers traveled northward over the sea ice, the remaining sled came closer and closer. Then the older brother cried, "Where is the one who will break the ice when our enemies are gaining on us?"

At once the younger boy raised his head and said, "I am here, my brother." Then he stretched out his finger and moved it as though he were drawing a line between the two sleds. As he moved it, the ice broke, and the sled coming up behind them was swallowed by the sea.

Early the next morning the brothers reached home and told their parents everything that had happened, how they had found the village, how they had met their sister, and how they had barely escaped with their lives. And that was the end. Never again did they journey southward.

And this ends, too. I do not know any more.

Canada and Greenland

The Dancing Fox

And now I am going to tell a story from times long ago. It is said that there was a boy lying unconscious on the sand. After a while he rose up and began to walk on the beach. He did not know where he was. He walked on and on, day after day, sleeping at night on the ground.

Winter was coming, and the boy found little to eat,

only a few roots and berries. He became weaker, and at last one day he sank down in a clump of grass, saying to himself, "I can't go any farther."

At that moment he saw a red fox walking toward him. When it came close, the boy took hold of it and began tapping its nose on the ground. The fox raised its head, the skin of its face folded back, and the fox's face became the face of a man.

Then the fox spoke, saying, "To the north only a short distance up the coast are many people. Let me take you there."

They started off at once, and when they arrived, the fox said, "Let me go ahead. You wait here."

While the boy waited, the fox ran into the village and shouted to the people, "Your enemies are coming! Many more than you! And they're almost here! Leave at once!"

The people were terrified. "This is the first time an animal has ever spoken to us," they cried. "We had better do what it says." Without stopping to pack their belongings, they all ran out of their houses, dashing through windows and doors with the speed of a shadow cast by the northern lights. They were never heard from again.

*"the fox said,
'Let me go ahead.
You wait here'"*

Calling to the boy, the fox said, "Everyone's gone now. You can come." Then the fox told him to pick out the best place he could find, and for a while the two stayed together and had an abundance of everything, skins to sleep on, meat to eat, everything that could be desired.

In the evenings the fox would entertain the boy. It would dance on its hind legs, going round and round, singing, "What a clever person I am!"

Then, when time had passed and the boy had grown older, the fox told him of a couple living inland with an unmarried daughter. "You are a man now," said the fox. "You must have a wife."

Then the fox walked inland to the house where the couple lived and called for someone to come out. A young woman appeared. As she stood there, astonished, the fox asked her if she would like to marry the two sons of a rich man.

"How can they be so rich as to send a red fox?" thought the young woman. But she said she would go inside and ask her father.

When the father came out, the fox said the same thing to him: "Won't you marry your daughter to the two sons of a rich man?"

"My daughter can do what she wants," replied the father. But at the same time he was thinking, "How rich those two men must be to send a talking fox to tell us!" Then he told his daughter to follow the fox.

And so she did. When she reached the village that the people had left, she saw only the young man. There was no one else in any of the houses. She and the young man were married, and the fox danced round and round on its hind legs. But the young woman knew that the fox had not told the truth.

The three of them lived together for a time. But at last the stored meat in the village was all used up, and the many skin robes that had once been fine were now soiled and torn.

Then the young man made preparations for fishing. He caught different kinds of fish whenever he could, and in this way he and his wife, though now poor, were able to live.

The fox, however, did not care to be poor and went inland to live somewhere else. When the fox came to the house where the young woman's parents lived, it stopped in and said, "There is no need to worry about your daughter. She is rich. She has everything she wants!" And it danced round and round on its hind legs.

From time to time the fox would pass by the old couple's house and would always stop in to say, "Your daughter has much more than you have here. Your daughter is rich!"

And that was the beginning of red foxes knowing how to make tricks against people and fooling them.

There, I have nothing more to tell.

Alaska

Little Bear

There was once an old woman who lived down below, close to the shore. Her house had only one window. She could do little more for herself than to gather snow for fresh water. But when the people who lived in the houses up above had been hunting, they gave her meat and blubber.

One evening when the hunters returned, they came

dragging a female bear. It was brought into one of the largest houses of the village to be butchered. When they opened it up, they found an unborn cub, all frozen.

The wife of the man who had shot the bear took the frozen cub to the poor old woman. She went up to the window of the house and cried, "Hello, dear friend in there! Wouldn't you like to have the bear's unborn cub?"

The old woman said yes, and she came out to get it.

Quickly she put a new moss wick in her lamp, lighted it so that it burned with a big flame, and laid the frozen bear on the drying rack above the lamp. There it thawed, and in a short time it began to move.

As soon as the old woman was sure that life was returning to the little bear's body, she took it down and laid it beside her. At last it opened its eyes.

It was just like a little puppy. Having long wished for just such a pet, she gave it her closest attention, as though it were a child, making it a soft warm bed alongside her own.

After it had begun to sleep next to her, it grew very fast, and she began to talk to it in human speech. That way it gained the mind of a human being. When it wished to ask the old woman for food, it would sniff, and then she would roast some blubber, for she had heard that bears lived on blubber. And that's how she fed it, giving it fried blubber to eat and melted blubber to drink.

When the cub would finish eating, the old woman would take it on her lap and sing to it:

Little one that will bring me snow when
　　you grow up,
Little one that will find meat for me when
　　you grow up.

Children from the village came every day to play with the bear cub. And in the old woman's house, which had once been lonely, there was life and happy days.

But the old woman warned the children about teasing the bear, and to the bear she said, "Bear child, little bear child, hide your claws well when you play with human children."

The bear grew and was big. Often, when playing, it accidentally broke the children's toy harpoons. It kept its claws in, however, and always took care not to hurt anyone.

*"the old woman
would take it
on her lap and
sing to it"*

At last it was so big that it was almost too rough and made the children cry. They became afraid of it, and from that time on the men of the village were the ones who played with the bear. They practiced different sports with it, so that its strength grew every day. But soon the men didn't dare continue. The bear's strength had become too great.

Then they said to each other, "Let us take it out hunting. It can help us catch seals at the blowholes."

One morning they came to the window and called, "Little bear, come out hunting with us and get your hunter's share."

When the bear heard this, it was eager to go with them. Soon it became more skilled than the men, catching even the largest of seals with a single blow of its paw.

Now the old woman had all the meat she could use.

When the weather was bad, the men stayed home. But the bear went out by itself and brought home seals for the whole village.

One time when the men had been out hunting with the bear, they called to the old woman as they passed her house, "Today your bear was nearly killed by the people living to the north of us. We were just able to save it."

Soon after, word came from a distant village to the south. People had heard of the bear and were saying, "If I ever see it, I will kill it."

Then the old woman's joy left her, and she was fearful every day. After thinking quietly for many days, she called her bear child to her and said, "Little bear, you have your own people far away, out where the ice floes drift along the outer shore. Go back to your people."

Crying, she dipped her hands in oil, smeared them with soot from the lamp, and marked the bear by stroking it along one side. Then the bear put its huge paw on her head for the last time and left the house. Walking slowly over the ice, it disappeared to the north.

The old woman stood outside her house until darkness fell, and all the neighbors watched her and felt her sadness. When they tried to comfort her, she merely whispered to herself, "Let people be people, and animals be animals. They cannot live together."

But it is not true that the bear was never heard of or seen again. People say that far to the north, when many bears are out on the ice, there will sometimes be seen in the distance a bear larger than all the others, with a dark spot on one side.

Canada and Greenland

The Great Giant Kinak

There was once an old hunter who was so ill-natured and resentful he could never rest and could not even sleep at night. He was angry all the time and treated everyone badly.

During the day his wife would send him out to bring back foods that were out of season—salmon, berries, whatever she could think of. She did this to keep him far from the house. But he always succeeded in getting quickly what he was sent for.

He was a fierce hunter of seals and would often come home with more than one. Sometimes he would catch an old male seal and would say to it, "Why do you come to me? I don't want to see your face. It reminds me too much of my own angry face." Then he would take the harpoon out of it and throw it back into the water.

One evening, when winter had set in, the hunter came home with a seal he had caught, and, as usual, before coming inside he gave the dogs a beating. He did this to quiet his temper, so he would not be in such a rage when he sat down to eat.

As soon as he entered the house, he told his wife to butcher the seal. She did so. And when she had finished cutting it up, she turned to him and said she was going outside to wash her hands with snow. Then she went out through the passageway, and the soles of her boots were the last he saw of her.

All through the dark winter night and for many days afterward the woman traveled toward the north. Finally she passed the last of the villages and left all signs of human life behind her. The cold became very intense, and she was now hungrier than she had ever been before. To ease her hunger pains she began to eat snow.

One day, as evening approached, she felt that she needed rest. But she had come to such a windswept place that she was unable to stop. She had no choice but to keep going. As she traveled on, she saw in the distance what seemed to be a hill with five peaks along the crest.

When she got close she saw that the hill had the shape of an enormous human foot. Climbing to the top of it, she removed the snow from between two peaks that looked like huge toes and found the place warm and comfortable. There she slept until morning.

When light came, she got up and walked on through level fields of snow until at last, when it grew dark again, she reached a hill that seemed to be shaped like a huge knee. Finding a sheltered spot next to it, she stayed there until morning, then continued on.

The next night she was sheltered in a round pitlike hollow, and when she left this place in the morning it appeared to her like a great navel.

The following night she came to a little valley, where she slept comfortably in a thicket of brushwood.

But in the morning, just as she was about to start out again, a great voice came from beneath her feet, saying, "Who are you?"

She was nearly overcome by fear. The voice spoke again: "What has driven you here, where human beings never come?"

Trembling, she managed to tell her story. Then the voice continued: "Well, you may stay here. But you must not sleep again between my lips and my chin or anywhere near my mouth, because if I breathed on you I would blow you away."

Then the voice became quieter. It said, "You must be hungry. I will get you something to eat."

While she was waiting, she suddenly realized that for the past three days she had been traveling on the body of the great giant Kinak. Then all at once the sky darkened, and a huge black cloud came swiftly toward her.

When it was almost on top of her, she saw that it was the giant's hand. As the hand opened, it dropped a freshly killed caribou. Then the voice told her to help herself.

As quickly as she could she gathered some of the

brushwood that grew all around, made a fire, and ate the roasted meat.

The giant spoke again: "Now you must find a place to hide, and it will be best for you to go into my beard where it is thickest, for I need to take a breath now and clear the frost that has gathered in my lungs. So hurry!"

She barely had time to get down into the giant's beard when a furious wind rushed over her head. Then a blinding snowstorm spread out over the tundra. It ended as quickly as it began, however, and the sky became clear once more.

The next day Kinak told her to find a good place to make a house, and after looking around she chose a spot on the left side of the giant's nose. There she built a hut, using hairs from his head.

For a long time she lived in the little hut, and whenever she needed food the giant reached out his hand and captured seals, caribou, and whatever else she wished for. From the skins of wolves, wolverines, and other animals that he caught she made herself beautiful clothing. Before long she had a great store of valuable skins and furs.

One day Kinak asked her if she would like to return home. "Yes," she replied, "but I am afraid of my husband. He treats me badly, and there is no one to protect me."

"I will protect you," said the giant. "Go and cut the ear tips from all the skins you have saved and put them in a basket. Then stand in front of my mouth. I will send you home, and whenever you are in danger remember to call, 'Kinak, Kinak, come to me!' And I will protect you. Go now. It is time. I have grown tired of lying so long in one place and wish to turn over, and if you were here you would be crushed."

She did as she was told and stood in front of the giant's mouth. Suddenly there was a great gust of wind with fine snow. The woman felt herself driven before it until she became sleepy and closed her eyes.

When she woke she was on the ground in her old village, and there beside her was the basket she had been carrying, now buried under a mound of valuable furs. Every ear tip had turned into a complete skin.

When her husband saw her, his pleasure was very great. He promised never to treat his wife badly again. And as for the furs, these beautiful skins made them the richest people in the village.

"'Yes,' she replied,
'but I am afraid of
my husband'"

After a while, however, the husband forgot his promise. Little by little he became unkind and harsh, just as before, until one day he became so enraged that he picked up a large stick to strike his wife.

Immediately she ran out of the house, crying, "Kinak, Kinak, come to me!" Her husband was close behind her. But scarcely had she said the words than a terrible blast of wind passed over her, blowing her husband away. He was never seen again.

The great giant Kinak, it is said, still lives in the north, although no one has been to him since. But whenever he breathes, the north winds of winter make his presence known.

Alaska

The Soul Wanderer

There was once a wifeless man whose name was Mako. He was a man of mighty strength, and, living alone, he not only did men's work but women's work, too, scraping the blubber from the insides of skins, stretching out the skins to dry, making mittens. There was nothing he could not do himself.

One day, when he had come back from hunting, he

noticed that the skin he had started cleaning the day before was half-finished, and his cooking pot was already boiling. All he had to do was turn the meat with a fork and finish scraping the skin.

The next day he came home and found two skins with the inner sides scraped clean. One of them even had the hair taken off. Again his pot was on the boil.

The following day he returned earlier than usual, and look! A beautiful woman was just going into the passageway. She wore a pair of white boots, and her hair was neatly arranged in a tuft on top of her head.

Mako ran up beside her and, taking hold of her hand, brought her into the house.

When autumn came, he brought his new wife with him to his winter village. There they settled down in the house of his cousins. One evening, just as Mako's wife had risen from her seat to go outside, a man sitting near the door remarked as she passed by, "What a strange odor!"

The man's housemates warned him not to offend their cousin's wife. But the same thing happened again. Someone asked, "What is that foxy odor?" This time the woman rushed from the house, barking like a fox, huk-huk-huk-huk, and as she passed the door curtain the people could see a long tail dangling at her back.

Mako ran crying after her, following her far into the hills. When he had lost sight of her, he followed her tracks until he came to a small hole in a mound of stones.

He stamped his foot over the foxhole and called down to her, "I feel so cold. Let me come in."

"Then come in," she said.

"But how?"

"Just breathe on the entrance and it will open wide." When he had entered, it seemed to him that he was in a real house, and his wife appeared to him in human form just as he had known her before.

"I feel so cold," he said.

Then she took him on her lap so that he sat across it as if he had been a little child. She rocked herself back and forth to lull him to sleep, first his body and then his soul. As she rocked, she sang this song:

Sleep, sleep,
And do not wake until summer is come.
Sleep, sleep,
And do not wake until the flies begin their
    humming.

*"Mako ran
crying after her,
following her far
into the hills"*

Sleep, sleep,

And do not wake until you hear the

rushing waters' sound.

Sleep, sleep,

And do not wake until the foxes begin

to bark among the hills.

Then he fell asleep and slept for a long time. When he woke, there was a humming of flies around the entrance to the burrow, and it was full summer. He walked outside, and there were grass and flowers. But now he was no longer a man. He was a spirit.

"What form shall I choose for my soul to wander in?" he asked himself. Then he crept into a blade of grass.

For a short time he remained in peace. But when the wind stirred, he swayed back and forth, and soon he became tired of the constant motion. Then he crept into the body of a raven.

Ravens never go hungry, as it seemed to him, but they often feel cold around their feet. And so he stopped being a raven and became a caribou.

He joined a herd of caribou, and they all moved off together. In their wanderings Mako was always behind the others. They asked him, "Why are you so slow?"

He answered, "I keep stumbling all the time." Then they told him how to look at the stars as he walked along. "Watching the ground makes you stumble," they said. After this, he followed their advice and was able to keep up with them.

"What shall I eat?" he asked.

"Scratch away the snow with your forefeet and find moss," they answered. Then he ate moss and grew fat.

One day the herd was attacked by a wolf, and all the caribou dashed into the sea. Mako ran with them, and when he reached the water his soul crept into the body of a walrus. He became hungry. He went down to the bottom of the sea to dig clams. But the clams would not open their shells, and he came up still hungry.

He said to the other walruses, "I can't get anything to eat. The clams refuse to open their shells for me."

The other walruses said, "When you get down to the bottom of the sea, say yock-yock-yock!" Then he went back to the bottom and said yock! The clams opened their shells, and he had all he wanted to eat. The others ate too.

After the walruses had eaten their fill, they climbed onto the rocks to rest. Mako went with them. Soon the others returned to the water, but Mako was tired of being a walrus, and he said to himself, "Now what form shall I choose for my soul to wander in?"

Just then a seal swam by, and Mako crept into it. For a long time he lived among the seals. One day, however, he looked to the shore and saw houses, and in one of the houses nearest the shore lived a woman who had not yet had a child.

Mako lay in wait for that woman's husband. One day he came up to breathe just in front of the place where the man was standing. The man harpooned him, and when he felt himself struck, he almost laughed aloud.

Now he was hauled ashore and brought into the house. They began to cut him up, and when the man threw his mittens to his wife, Mako went with the mittens and crept into the body of the woman. After a time he was born again as the woman's child.

Then they had to find a name for him, and at first they called him after a dead relative. They did not call him Mako. And hearing a strange name, he began to cry.

One day his father, who was very fond of him and looked after him, heard him saying, "I am Mako." The father was so astonished that he nearly dropped him. "Ha!" said the father. "He wants to be named after that Mako who was lost in the hills. He is Mako!"

Then the child stopped crying and entered upon his human life once again. When he had grown to be an old man, it became a story. And those who came after him constantly told it further.

Now it is finished. I don't know any more.

Alaska, Canada, and Greenland

Two Dried Fish

There was a married couple who lived in a house with their relatives. Although the house was filled with children, the couple had none of their own. They just hoped. Their hopes, however, were in vain.

After a time the husband became silent, then very silent. And this no doubt was because he could get no children.

When summer came, he paddled away in his kayak as far as he could to the north, hoping to find something that would change his luck.

The next summer he paddled as far as he could to the south, and when he had almost given up hope he came to an old woman who promised to help him. Reaching into her bag, she pulled out two small dried fish, a male and a female.

The first of these she handed to the man, saying, "Let your wife eat this if you want a son." Then she gave him the second and said, "She will eat this if you prefer a daughter."

The man took the male fish and the female fish and headed for home. But the journey was far, and he was not always able to find food. At last, when he was hungrier than usual, he said to himself, "Why keep both of these fish? A son is what we desire." And with that he swallowed the female fish.

After a while he began to feel ill at ease. At the same time he was growing bigger and bigger, and at last he could hardly manage to slip down into his kayak.

At a place where he happened to land, there was another old woman known to be wise. The woman looked at him carefully, and soon she suspected what

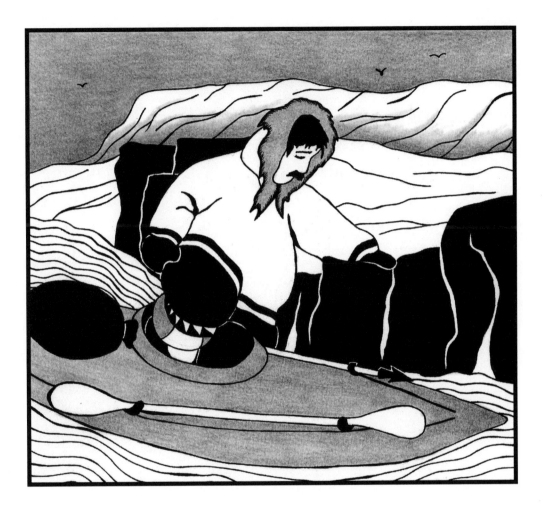

*"at last he could
hardly manage
to slip down into
his kayak"*

was the matter. Then she hit on a charm and recited these words:

> Let her come out!
> There is one who wishes
>   to come out!

And look! An infant appeared.

And later, when the man returned to his wife, he was carrying with him a beautiful daughter.

And here it ends. I don't know any more.

Greenland

The Blind Boy
and the Loon

A long long time ago, a boy and a girl lived with their stepmother in a small house. When the boy was still growing, he made a bow and some arrows out of walrus tusks and shot birds, which they all ate.

One day at the beginning of winter the boy came home with a young seal. As he dragged it into the house, his stepmother claimed the skin for herself, saying she had to have it as a cover for her sleeping platform.

But the boy needed the skin for rawhide cords to make a harpoon line. He insisted, and the stepmother became angry. Later, as she was cleaning the skin and removing the hair, she worked magic on it and spoke to it in these words:

When he cuts you
    into cords,
When he cuts you
    with his knife,
Jump up,
    strike him back,
And snap him
    in the face.

Then she was satisfied, thinking of what would happen.

When she had finished cleaning the skin, she gave it to the boy, and he cut the first cord. Then he stretched it tight. But just as he began to scrape it with a shell, the cord broke in two, snapping against his face and blinding him in both eyes.

From that moment, his stepmother treated him

"as she was
cleaning the skin
and removing the
hair, she worked
magic on it"

badly in every possible way. She never gave him enough to eat and would not allow his sister to give him anything at all.

Now winter was coming on, and they had no way of getting meat. They had to live entirely on the shellfish. Since the boy could no longer hunt, he sat in the house all day long.

One day a bear appeared at the window. The sister and the stepmother, out of fear, ran to the far side of the room. Then the boy called to his sister, "Bring me my bow."

Already the bear had eaten part of the window skin and was thrusting its head into the house. The boy bent the bow and told his sister to aim it for him. Carefully she leveled it. Then, just as she gave the signal, he shot, and the bear fell backward, tumbling into the snow.

"You only hit the window frame," said the stepmother immediately.

But the sister whispered to him, "You killed a bear."

When the stepmother had skinned the bear, there was plenty of good rich meat for the days ahead. But the boy never tasted a single meal from his own hunting. The stepmother kept him at the point of starving, giving him only a few shellfish.

Sometimes the sister would hide a piece of meat in her sleeve and give it to her brother when they were alone in the house. He would have to swallow it quickly before the stepmother came back inside.

And so the winter passed. At last the days lengthened, and one morning, when it was spring, the sister turned to her brother and said, "Do you remember what good times we used to have when you could still see, and how we used to walk around the country?"

"Yes," answered the brother, "let's go now. I can take hold of you."

Then they set out together and wandered all day long, the boy holding on to his sister's sleeve, while she gathered shrubs for fuel.

Before long they came to a large lake. The boy said, "I think I'll sit here and rest, while you look for more firewood."

As soon as he was alone, he heard a voice saying, "Come!" Slowly he made his way to the shore of the lake. He felt his hand being taken by the hand of another person. It was a loon. It had called to him, and now it was leading him into the water.

The loon said, "Put your arms around my neck and I will dive with you to the bottom of the lake."

They stayed underwater for a long time. When they came up, the bird asked him, "Can you see now?"

"No, I cannot see," he replied.

Then the bird dived with him again and stayed underwater longer. When they came to the surface, the loon asked him again, "Can you see?"

"I can see a shimmer of light," he said.

Again they dived to the bottom of the lake, and now they stayed under a very long time. When they came back up, the boy opened his eyes wide and could see everything around him. He thanked the loon, and the loon told him to go back to his stepmother's house and see what he could see.

When he returned home with his sister, he found the skin of the bear he had shot, drying in the warm rays of the sun. He entered the house and asked his stepmother, "Where did you get the bearskin?"

Realizing the boy was no longer blind, the stepmother became frightened. She lied to him. "I got it from some people who were passing by," she said. "They gave it to me."

The boy made no reply, and in the days that followed he went back to his hunting and brought home seals. Then he went to the other people in the village and asked them to help him make a harpoon line and a harpoon. In a short time he became an expert hunter of white whales.

One day, when he was about to go whale hunting, he asked his stepmother to come with him and hold the harpoon line. She agreed, and when they got to the shore, he told her to tie the line around her waist, while he threw the harpoon.

Soon the white whales began coming to the surface. The stepmother became worried and cried, "Take one of the smallest!" But seeing an unusually large one, the boy speared it with his harpoon, and as it swam away it dragged the stepmother into the sea.

She disappeared under the waves, then came up again. And whenever she reappeared she could be heard crying luke-luke-luke! Gradually she was changed into a narwhale, and her long hair, spread out behind her, became twisted round and round in a spiral—which is why the narwhale today has a twisted tusk.

So that was her end. And the end of this, too.

Alaska, Canada, and Greenland

Notes

Works here identified by author and short title or by a two-letter abbreviation (BC, BE, CN, etc.) will be found fully listed in the References.

Introduction

Page ix / folktales published in Canada: McGrath, *Canadian Inuit Literature,* pp. 76-77. *Page xi* / "Each hamlet had its great narrator ": TA, p. 387. *Page xi* / "gesticulation, shouting, and modulation of the voice": HL, p. 229. *Page xi* / "You ruin our stories": Rasmussen, *Eagle's Gift,* p. vi. *Page xii* / storytelling in total darkness: MT, p. 11. *Page xii* / storyteller with face turned toward the wall: BC, p. 164. *Page xii* / storyteller's helper laid out sticks: NE, p. 451. *Page xii* / two kinds of narratives: RT, p. 83; OG, p. 4; Edna MacLean, Alaska Native Language Center (private communication). *Page xiii* / shortening the winter: HL, p. 270; OG, p. 4. *Page xvi* / umiak rowed by women: Bruemmer, "Last of the Umiaks," pp. 42-44. *Page xvii* / snow house construction: BC, pp. 132-33. *Page xx* / domesticated caribou drink from buckets: HL, p. 237. *Page xxi* / shamans' visits to undersea woman: Damas, *Handbook,* p. 633; BC, pp. 175-80; McGrath, *Canadian Inuit Literature,* p. 70. *Page xxiii* / Rink and Boas combined texts to produce a single version: RT, pp. 93-288; BC, p. 175. *Page xxv* / proposed province of Nunavut: *New York Times,* Feb. 28, 1976 ("Eskimos Seek Fifth of Canada as Province"), Dec. 17, 1991 ("Accord to Give Eskimos Control of a Fifth of Canada"), and Dec. 19, 1991 ("Correction" on p. A13). *Page xxv* / Home Rule Act for Greenland: Damas, *Handbook,* pp. 620, 715-16, 726. *Page xxv* / Inuit Circumpolar Conference: Damas, *Handbook,* pp. 724-28; M. Stenbaek, Centre for Northern Studies, McGill University (private communication).

Stories

Page 3 / The Adventures of Kivio. Variants: Canada (BC, p. 213; BE, p. 182; RC, p. 97; RE, p. 237; RI, p. 287; RN, p. 365; RN, p. 523); Greenland (OG, p. 52; RP, p. 195; RT, p. 157). Sources for this version: BC, BE, OG, RC, RN, and RT; with details from OG, p. 33; OG, p. 60; HL, p. 257; NE, p. 512; RP, pp. 205-6; RT, p. 366; RT, p. 429; TA, p. 415; and TA, p. 425.

Also called Kiviok, Kiviung (BC), or Kiviuna (RE), the hero is one of the best-known figures in Arctic folklore. Superhuman in his strength and cleverness, he is considered to be immortal; or, as some say, he has had many lives and is now living his last one (RN). In modern Canada he has appeared in a comic strip (McGrath, *Canadian Inuit Literature,* p. 71).

Page 12 / The Woman Under the Sea. Source: RT, p. 324; with details from HL, pp. 249-50; OG, p. 42; RA, p. 38; RA, p. 75; RT, p. 238; RT, p. 259; RT, pp. 281-85, and Ostermann, *Life and Doings,* p. 175.

The undersea woman who releases food animals is known only from Canada and Greenland. According to a different tradition, known throughout the American Arctic, the animals are sent to earth from above by the moon man (BE, p. 198; NE, p. 515; RP, p. 174). Stories about shamans who visit the undersea woman differ too greatly to be called variants of one another, although many of the incidents are found widely in Inuit lore. In eastern Canada the woman has been given the name Sedna.

Page 20 / A Giant and Her Little Son. Variants: Canada (BC, p. 230; BE, p. 196; JM, p. 83; OM, p. 76; RE, p. 218; SE, p. 74); Greenland (HL, p. 232). Source for this version: BE; with details from BC, HL, and JM.

In some variants the giant is male; in others, female. His or her companion is sometimes a husband, sometimes (as here) an adopted son. Notice that the giant calls the boy "Little Legs," a name used in folktales by supernaturals when referring to a human being. Compare JM, p. 58 ("Small Calves"); SE, p. 21 ("Little Shins").

Page 26 / The Lost Boys. Source: CN, p. 179.

The story of the two lost boys and their shaman grandmother is from the Kotzbue Sound region of northwestern Alaska. Like many Alaskan Inuit tales it does not appear to have variants in Canada or Greenland.

Page 35 / Worms and Lice. Variants: Canada (RN, p. 412); Greenland (OG, p. 117; RP, p. 161). Sources for this version: OG, RP.

Although women usually did the paddling when family groups traveled by umiak, the louse husband in this case evidently expects to be handling the oars. This is why he needs mittens–an essential item for rowing. On long journeys by umiak or kayak, one might even take extra pairs (as does the hero in "The Adventures of Kivio").

Page 39 / The Girls Who Wished for Husbands. Variants: Alaska (SN, p. 386); Canada (BE, p. 217; BE, p. 317; JM, p. 77; OM, p. 117; RC, p. 94; RE, p. 221; RI, p. 281; RN, p. 409); Greenland (HL, p. 259; KT, p. 175; OG, p. 124; RA, p. 130; RT, p. 126). Sources for this version: BE, JM, RA, RT, SN; with details from BE, p. 192.

The tale is known from Greenland to Alaska, and a variant has been reported from eastern Siberia (Bogoras, "Folklore," p. 607). Even more widespread is the episode known to folklorists as the "magic flight" or "obstacle flight" (Leach and Fried, *Dictionary,* p. 811), which appears in traditional tales the world over and probably reached the American Arctic by way of Asia (Thompson, *Tales,* pp. 333-34). In our story a hairband and two mittens serve as the magic obstacles that aid the girl in her flight from the whale.

Page 46 / The Orphan Who Became Strong. Variants: Alaska (OA, p. 188); Canada (AS, p. 73; BC, p. 220; BC, p. 222; BE, p. 186; BE, p. 309; BE, p. 519; MT, p. 35; OM, p. 99; RC, p. 96; RN, p. 418);

Greenland (OG, p. 67; OG, p. 73; RA, p. 117; RP, p. 201; RT, p. 93). Sources for this version: BC, BE, OG, RP, RT; with details from BE, p. 182; HL, p. 255; NE, p. 490; OG, p. 290; RN, p. 432; RP, p. 181; RT, p. 98; RT, p. 308.

The orphan boy is one of the most interesting characters in Inuit folklore, appearing not only in the tale given here but in many other kinds of stories. As a fictional character he is despised and often cruelly intimidated. But while the male orphan in childhood may be an unwanted burden, he becomes a supporter and an essential asset in the time of his adoptive parent's old age.

Page 55 / Two Sisters and Their Caribou Husbands. Source: RT, p. 169; with details from OA, p. 262; OG, p. 75; LS, pp. 267–68; RE, p. 115; RP, p. 188; RP, p. 198; RT, p. 114; RT, p. 289.

The marriage of a human being to an animal is one of the major themes in Inuit and American Indian folklore. The underlying idea in many of the stories is that an animal wife or husband enriches the human community by establishing a connection to nature, the ultimate source of livelihood. Although the relationship may be dangerous, it permits the hunter (either as spouse or as in-law) to know the ways of animals and to hunt them more successfully than would otherwise be possible.

Page 63 / The Land of the Birds. Variants: Alaska (SN, p. 391); Canada (BC, p. 207; BE, p. 179; JM, p. 49; RE, p. 230; RI, p. 265; RN, p. 373; RN, p. 524); Greenland (KT, p. 170; RP, p. 165; RT, p. 145). Sources for this version: BC, BE, RI, RC, RN, RP, RT; with details from RP, p. 190.

Here again, as in the preceding, is a tale of human-animal marriage. Better known as "The Swan Maidens" or "The Goose Wife," the story of the man who journeys to the land of the birds is perhaps the most famous example of a folktale that is native to the entire world. Deeply entrenched in Inuit tradition, it also belongs to the folklore of North America south of the Arctic, South America, Europe,

Africa, Asia, Australia, and Oceania. See Leach and Fried, *Dictionary,* pp. 1091–92; Aarne and Thompson, *Types,* nos. 313, 400, and 465.

Page 70 / Kasiak. Variants: Canada (MT, p. 113); Greenland (OG, p. 46; RA, p. 123; RP, p. 187; RT, p. 291; TA, p. 440). Source for this version: RT; with details from OG, RA, RP, TA.

Two trickster figures are prominent in Inuit folklore: the bumbling Kasiak of Greenland (known in Canada as the lazy son-in-law) and the malicious fox of Alaska and Canada. Tricksters in native American lore are usually animals; or if they are fully human, as here, they often have an animal namesake. The name Kasiak, or its variant Qasigiaq, means pied seal (RP, p. 187), also called harp seal or saddleback seal.

Page 78 / The Woman Who Lived by Herself. Source: HL, p. 251; with details from BC, p. 220; BE, p. 216; OG, p. 74; RN, p. 432.

The story has no actual variant, but Inuit tales in which women live apart from men and provide for themselves are frequent in Arctic folklore. "Two Sisters and Their Caribou Husbands" offers one example; others are in BC, p. 220 (two pregnant women flee their husbands and live by themselves), and RT, p. 420 (a deserted woman and her adopted daughter become their own providers).

Page 84 / Cannibal Village. Variants: Canada (JM, p. 86; RI, p. 291); Greenland (OG, p. 39; RT, p. 128). Sources for this version: OG, RT; with details from BE, p. 192; BE, p. 205; BE, p. 208; BE, pp. 312–13; BE, p. 203; JM; RP, p. 186.

As in all cultures the role of the habitual cannibal, or ogre, belongs to fantasy rather than fact. Needless to say, there have never been cannibal villages in the Arctic. But lively tales of such communities—and of babies who ate their parents and of hungry husbands who fattened their wives—were standard fare for the storytellers' audiences during the long winter evenings.

Page 92 / The Dancing Fox. Source: SN, p. 395; with details from JM, p. 44; JM, p. 56; OG, p. 33.

In Arctic folklore the fox is a cruel trickster who usually plays pranks on other animals. Here his malice is directed toward humans—among whom only the young woman seems fully aware of what is happening. Notice that the fox promises the woman not one but two husbands, an arrangement not unheard of in Inuit society and one that implies high status and material comforts for the woman.

Page 98 / Little Bear. Variants: Canada (BC, p. 230; BE, p. 222; RN, p. 407); Greenland (HL, p. 290; OG, p. 129; OG, p. 137; RA, p. 40). Sources for this version: OG; with details from BC; RA; RI, p. 268; RN.

Although the black bear and the grizzly bear are known in the western half of the American Arctic, the usual bear of Inuit folktales (as here) is the white-furred polar bear, in maturity attaining a length of seven-and-a-half feet and weighing up to eleven hundred pounds.

Page 105 / The Great Giant Kinak. Source: NE, p. 471; with details from BE, p. 191; BE, p. 235; BE, p. 285; BE, p. 536; RT, p. 112.

The giants of Arctic folklore are often of colossal proportions, and Kinak, whose body seems to merge with the earth itself, is perhaps the greatest of them all. Giants are sometimes said to sleep all winter and wake in spring, suggesting that they are earth spirits. Compare "The Giant and Her Little Son," above.

Page 113 / The Soul Wanderer. Variants: Alaska (NE, p. 505); Canada (BE, p. 232); Greenland (HL, p. 272; OG, p. 22; RA, p. 100; RT, p. 450; TA, p. 409). Source for this version: OG, p. 22; with details from BE, pp. 225–26; BE, p. 233; BE, p. 322; HL; JM, p. 58; OG, p. 77; RA, p. 102; RT, p. 145; RT, pp. 427–28; TA.

The tale of the soul that wanders from plant to animal and from animal to animal, finally to be born again as a human, is told of both men and women. In the version given here, the wanderer is a man, whose adventures as a soul are preceded by a folkloric episode that may be called "The Fox Wife." Often told as a separate tale, "The Fox Wife" has these variants: Canada (BE, p. 222; JM, p. 76; SE, p. 64); Greenland (OG, p. 22; OG, p. 120; RT, p. 143). "The Soul Wanderer" and "The Fox Wife" are joined, as here, in OG, p. 22.

Page 121 / Two Dried Fish. Source: RT, p. 443; with details from RA, p. 20; TA, p. 413; TA, p. 441.

Although the story was collected in Greenland from an Inuit storyteller and has acquired an Inuit flavor, its ultimate origin must be traced to Europe. In Danish and other variants the infant is said to have been born from the man's knee. As told in Europe the tale gives rise to a riddle: a fish was my father, a man was my mother (Aarne and Thompson, *Types,* no. 705).

Page 125 / The Blind Boy and the Loon. Variants: Alaska (SN, p. 396); Canada (BC, p. 217; BE, p. 168; MT, p. 92; NU, p. 48; RC, p. 108; RE, p. 204; RN, p. 524; SE, p. 48); Greenland (HL, p. 250; RP, p. 169; RT, p. 99). Sources for this version: BC, BE, HE, RT, SN; with details from SE; TA, p. 425.

The widespread tale of the blind boy and his cruel stepmother belongs not only to Inuit tradition but to the American Indian folklore of western Canada, the Plains, and the Great Basin (Thompson, *Tales,* p. 354). In a few of the Greenland variants the loon is replaced by a goose.

References

A. Folktale Sources

AS   Alivatuk, Jamasie, et al. *Stories from Pangnirtung* (foreword by Stuart Hodgson). Edmonton, Alberta: Hurtig, 1976.

BC   Boas, Franz. *The Central Eskimo.* Lincoln: University of Nebraska Press, 1964 (originally published 1888).

BE   ——. *The Eskimo of Baffin Land and Hudson Bay.* Bulletin of the American Museum of Natural History 15. New York, 1901-1907.

CN   Curtis, Edward S. *The North American Indian,* vol. 20. New York: Johnson Reprint, 1970 (originally published 1930).

Hall, Edwin S., Jr. *The Eskimo Storyteller: Folktales from Noatak, Alaska.* Knoxville: University of Tennessee Press, 1975.

HL   Holm, Gustav. "Legends and Tales from Angmagsalik." In William Thalbitzer, ed., *The Ammassalik Eskimo,* vol. 1, pp. 225-306. New York: AMS, 1979 (originally published 1914).

JM   Jenness, Diamond. *Myths and Traditions from Northern Alaska, the Mackenzie Delta, and Coronation Gulf.* Report of the Canadian Arctic Expedition 1913-18, vol. 13(A). Ottawa, 1924.

KT   Kroeber, Alfred. "Tales of the Smith Sound Eskimo," *Journal of American Folklore* 12(46): pp. 166-82.

LS   Lantis, Margaret. "The Social Culture of the Nunivak Eskimo," *Transactions of the American Philosophical Society* n.s. 35(3): pp. 153-323. Philadelphia, 1946.

Lowenstein, Thomas. *The Things That Were Said of Them: Shaman Stories and Oral Histories of the Tikigaq People.* Berkeley: University of California Press, 1992.

MT   Metayer, Maurice. *Tales from the Igloo.* Edmonton, Alberta: Hurtig, 1972.

NE   Nelson, Edward W. "The Eskimo about Bering Strait," *18th Annual Report of the Bureau of American Ethnology for the Years*

1896–97, pp. 3–518. Washington, 1899.

NU Nungak, Zebedee, and Eugene Arima. *Unikkaatuat sanau-garngnik atyingualit Puvirngniturngmit: Eskimo Stories from Povungnituk, Quebec.* Anthropological Series 90, National Museum of Canada Bulletin 235. Ottawa, 1969.

OA Ostermann, Hother, ed. *The Alaskan Eskimos, as Described in the Posthumous Notes of Dr. Knud Rasmussen.* Copenhagen: Gyldendal, 1952.

OG ——, ed. *Knud Rasmussen's Posthumous Notes on East Greenland Legends and Myths.* Copenhagen: C.A. Reitzel, 1939.

OM ——, ed. *The Mackenzie Eskimos after Knud Rasmussen's Posthumous Notes.* Copenhagen: Gyldendal, 1942.

RA Rasmussen, Knud. *Eskimo Folk-Tales.* W. Worster, ed. and trans. London and Copenhagen: Gyldendal, 1921.

RC ——. *Intellectual Culture of the Caribou Eskimos.* Copenhagen: Gyldendal, 1930.

RE ——. *Intellectual Culture of the Copper Eskimos.* Copenhagen: Gyldendal, 1932.

RI ——. *Intellectual Culture of the Iglulik Eskimos.* Copenhagen: Gyldendal, 1929.

RN ——. *Intellectual Culture of the Netsilik Eskimos.* Copenhagen: Gyldendal, 1931.

RP ——. *The People of the Polar North.* Philadelphia: Lippincott, 1908.

RT Rink, Hinrich J. *Tales and Traditions of the Eskimo.* New York, 1975 (originally published 1875).

SE Spalding, Alex. *Eight Inuit Myths.* Canadian Ethnology Service, Paper 59. Ottawa: National Museum of Canada, 1979.

SN Spencer, Robert F. *The North Alaskan Eskimo.* New York: Dover, 1976 (originally published 1959).

TA Thalbitzer, William. "Language and Folklore." In Thalbitzer, ed., *The Ammassalik Eskimo,* vol. 2, pp. 113–495. New York: AMS, 1979 (originally published 1923).

B. Other Works

Aarne, Antti, and Stith Thompson. *The Types of the Folktale.* 2d rev. Helsinki: Suomalainen Tiedeakatemia, 1973.

Bogoras, Waldemar. "The Folklore of Northeastern Asia, as Compared with that of Northwestern America," *American Anthropologist* 4 (1902): pp. 577–683.

Bruemmer, Fred. "Last of the Umiaks," *Natural History,* Oct. 1992, pp. 40–47.

Damas, David. *Handbook of North American Indians,* vol. 5 (Arctic). Washington: Smithsonian, 1984.

Leach, Maria, and Jerome Fried. *Standard Dictionary of Folklore, Mythology, and Legend.* New York: Funk & Wagnalls, 1972.

McGrath, Robin. *Canadian Inuit Literature.* Canadian Ethnology Service, Paper 94. Ottawa: National Museums of Canada, 1984.

Ostermann, Hother, ed. *Knud Rasmussen's Posthumous Notes on the Life and Doings of the East Greenlanders in Olden Times.* Copenhagen: C.A. Reitzel, 1938.

Rasmussen, Knud. *The Eagle's Gift.* New York: Doubleday, Doran & Co., 1936.

Thompson, Stith. *Tales of the North American Indians.* Bloomington: Indiana University Press, 1966.